EOIN COLFER

ARTEMIS FOWL

THE ARCTIC INCIDENT

THE GRAPHIC NOVEL

Adapted by **Michael Moreci**
Art by **Stephen Gilpin**

Disney • HYPERION

Los Angeles   New York

Adapted from the novel *The Arctic Incident*

Text copyright © 2021 by Eoin Colfer

Illustrations copyright © 2021 Disney Enterprises, Inc.

First Hardcover Edition, March 2021
First Paperback Edition, March 2021

10 9 8 7 6 5 4 3 2 1

FAC-038091-21015
Printed in the United States of America

This book is set in Colleen Doran/Fontspring; DIN Next LT Pro, ITC Novarese Pro,
Neutraface Condensed/Monotype

Designed by Stephen Gilpin and Tyler Nevins

Library of Congress Cataloging-in-Publication Data

Names: Moreci, Michael, adapter. • Gilpin, Stephen, artist. • Colfer, Eoin, author.
Artemis Fowl.
Title: Artemis Fowl, the arctic incident : the graphic novel / adapted by
Michael Moreci ; art by Stephen Gilpin.
Other titles: Arctic incident
Description: Los Angeles ; New York : Disney-Hyperion, 2021. • Series: Artemis Fowl ;
2 • Sequel to: *Artemis Fowl.* • Audience: Ages 8–12 • Audience: Grades
4–6 • Summary: "A full-color graphic novel adaptation of the
internationally best-selling book about a twelve-year-old criminal
mastermind and the world of fairies"—Provided by publisher.
Identifiers: LCCN 2019056129 (print) • LCCN 2019056130 (ebook) •
ISBN 9781368064705 (hardcover) • ISBN 9781368065306 (paperback) •
ISBN 9781368065368 (ebook) •
Subjects: LCSH: Graphic novels. • CYAC: Graphic novels. • Fairies—Fiction.
• Kidnapping—Fiction. • Magic—Fiction.
Classification: LCC PZ7.7.M658 Ar 2021 (print) • LCC PZ7.7.M658 (ebook) •
DDC 741.5/942—dc23
LC record available at https://lccn.loc.gov/2019056129
LC ebook record available at https://lccn.loc.gov/2019056130

Visit www.DisneyBooks.com

To Ferdia and Lara for all their
hard work and talent.
—E.C.

For my family, who remind me every
day why I love telling stories.
—M.M.

For Jen
—S.G.

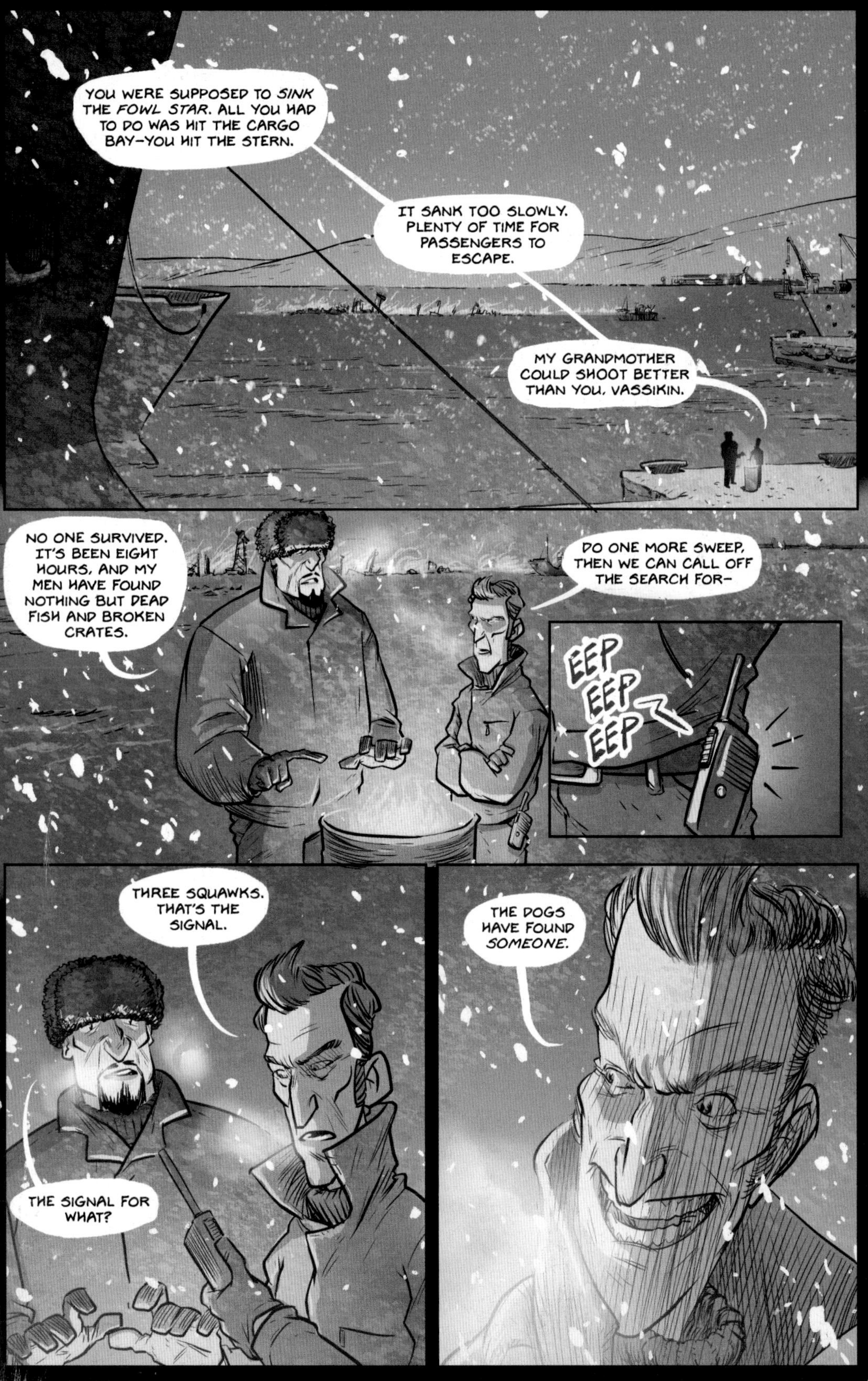
YOU WERE SUPPOSED TO *SINK* THE *FOWL STAR*. ALL YOU HAD TO DO WAS HIT THE CARGO BAY—YOU HIT THE STERN.
IT SANK TOO SLOWLY. PLENTY OF TIME FOR PASSENGERS TO ESCAPE.
MY GRANDMOTHER COULD SHOOT BETTER THAN YOU, VASSIKIN.
NO ONE SURVIVED. IT'S BEEN EIGHT HOURS, AND MY MEN HAVE FOUND NOTHING BUT DEAD FISH AND BROKEN CRATES.
DO ONE MORE SWEEP, THEN WE CAN CALL OFF THE SEARCH FOR–
EEP EEP EEP
THREE SQUAWKS. THAT'S THE SIGNAL.
THE SIGNAL FOR WHAT?
THE DOGS HAVE FOUND *SOMEONE*.

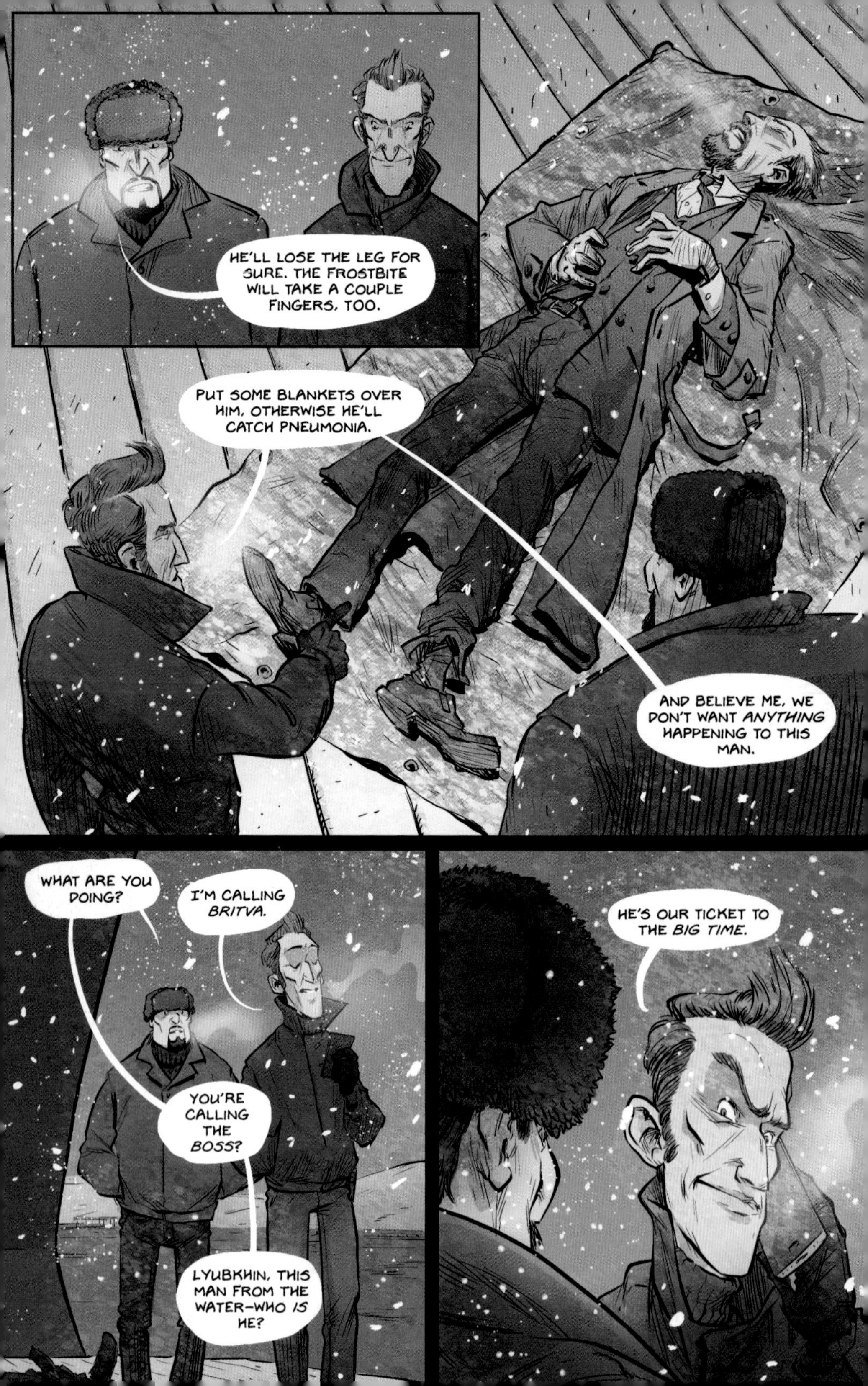
HE'LL LOSE THE LEG FOR SURE. THE FROSTBITE WILL TAKE A COUPLE FINGERS, TOO.
PUT SOME BLANKETS OVER HIM, OTHERWISE HE'LL CATCH PNEUMONIA.
AND BELIEVE ME, WE DON'T WANT *ANYTHING* HAPPENING TO THIS MAN.
WHAT ARE YOU DOING?
I'M CALLING *BRITVA.*
YOU'RE CALLING THE *BOSS?*
LYUBKHIN, THIS MAN FROM THE WATER—WHO *IS* HE?
HE'S OUR TICKET TO THE *BIG TIME.*

CHAPTER ONE

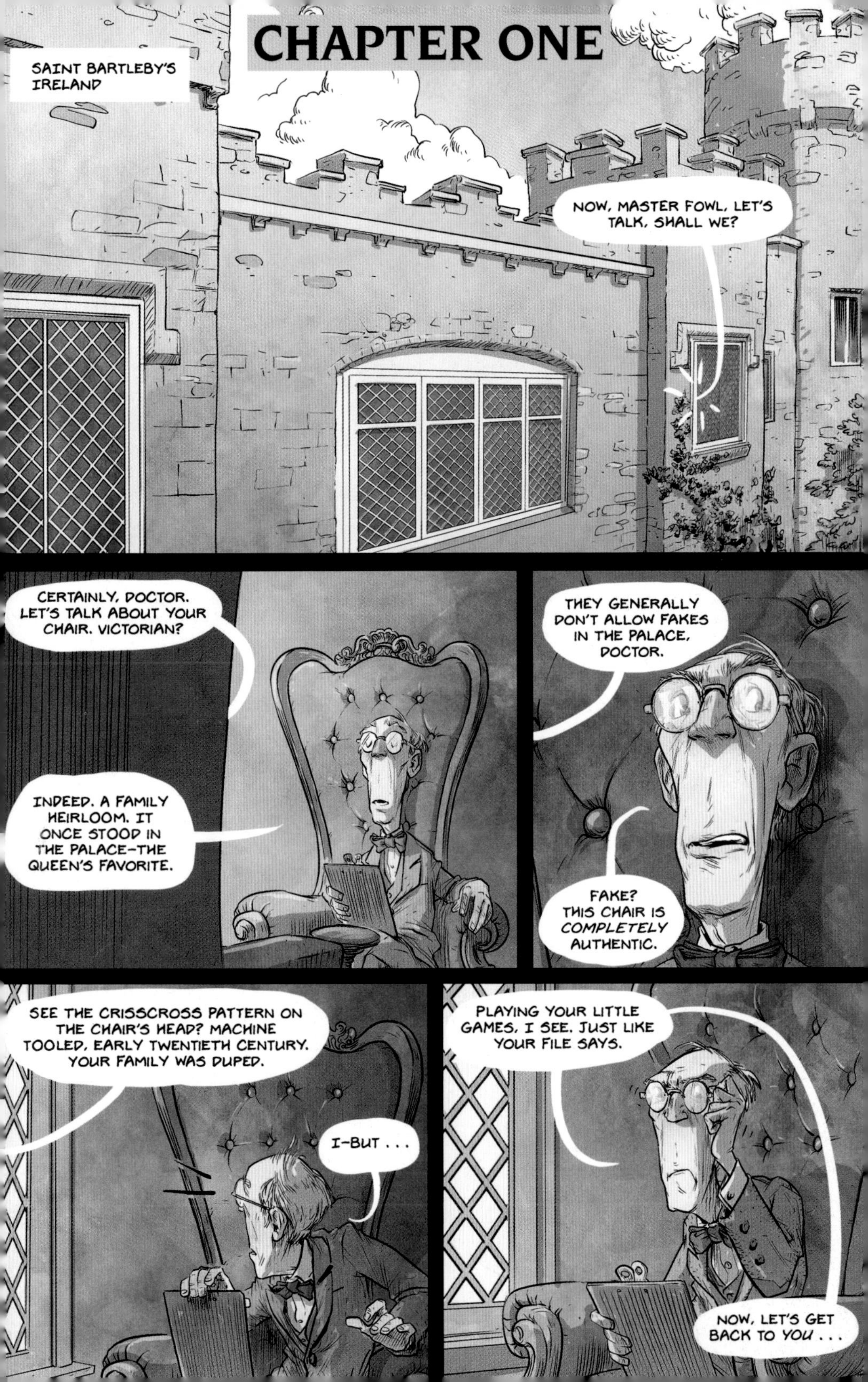
SAINT BARTLEBY'S IRELAND
NOW, MASTER FOWL, LET'S TALK, SHALL WE?
CERTAINLY, DOCTOR. LET'S TALK ABOUT YOUR CHAIR. VICTORIAN?
INDEED. A FAMILY HEIRLOOM. IT ONCE STOOD IN THE PALACE—THE QUEEN'S FAVORITE.
THEY GENERALLY DON'T ALLOW FAKES IN THE PALACE, DOCTOR.
FAKE? THIS CHAIR IS *COMPLETELY* AUTHENTIC.
SEE THE CRISSCROSS PATTERN ON THE CHAIR'S HEAD? MACHINE TOOLED, EARLY TWENTIETH CENTURY. YOUR FAMILY WAS DUPED.
I—BUT . . .
PLAYING YOUR LITTLE GAMES, I SEE. JUST LIKE YOUR FILE SAYS.
NOW, LET'S GET BACK TO *YOU* . . .

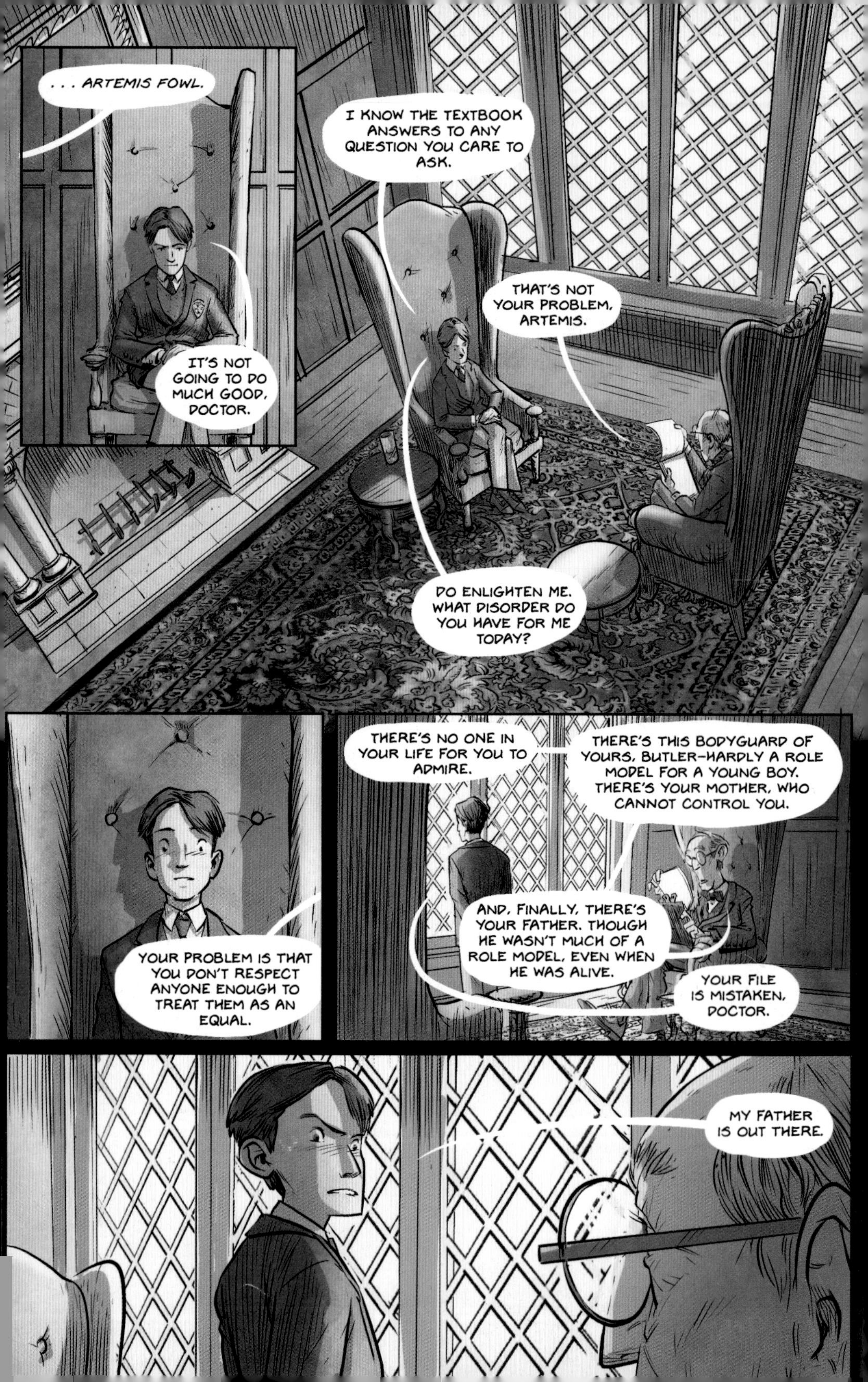

. . . ARTEMIS FOWL.
IT'S NOT GOING TO DO MUCH GOOD, DOCTOR.
I KNOW THE TEXTBOOK ANSWERS TO ANY QUESTION YOU CARE TO ASK.
THAT'S NOT YOUR PROBLEM, ARTEMIS.
DO ENLIGHTEN ME. WHAT DISORDER DO YOU HAVE FOR ME TODAY?
YOUR PROBLEM IS THAT YOU DON'T RESPECT ANYONE ENOUGH TO TREAT THEM AS AN EQUAL.
THERE'S NO ONE IN YOUR LIFE FOR YOU TO ADMIRE.
THERE'S THIS BODYGUARD OF YOURS, BUTLER–HARDLY A ROLE MODEL FOR A YOUNG BOY. THERE'S YOUR MOTHER, WHO CANNOT CONTROL YOU.
AND, FINALLY, THERE'S YOUR FATHER. THOUGH HE WASN'T MUCH OF A ROLE MODEL, EVEN WHEN HE WAS ALIVE.
YOUR FILE IS MISTAKEN, DOCTOR.
MY FATHER IS OUT THERE.

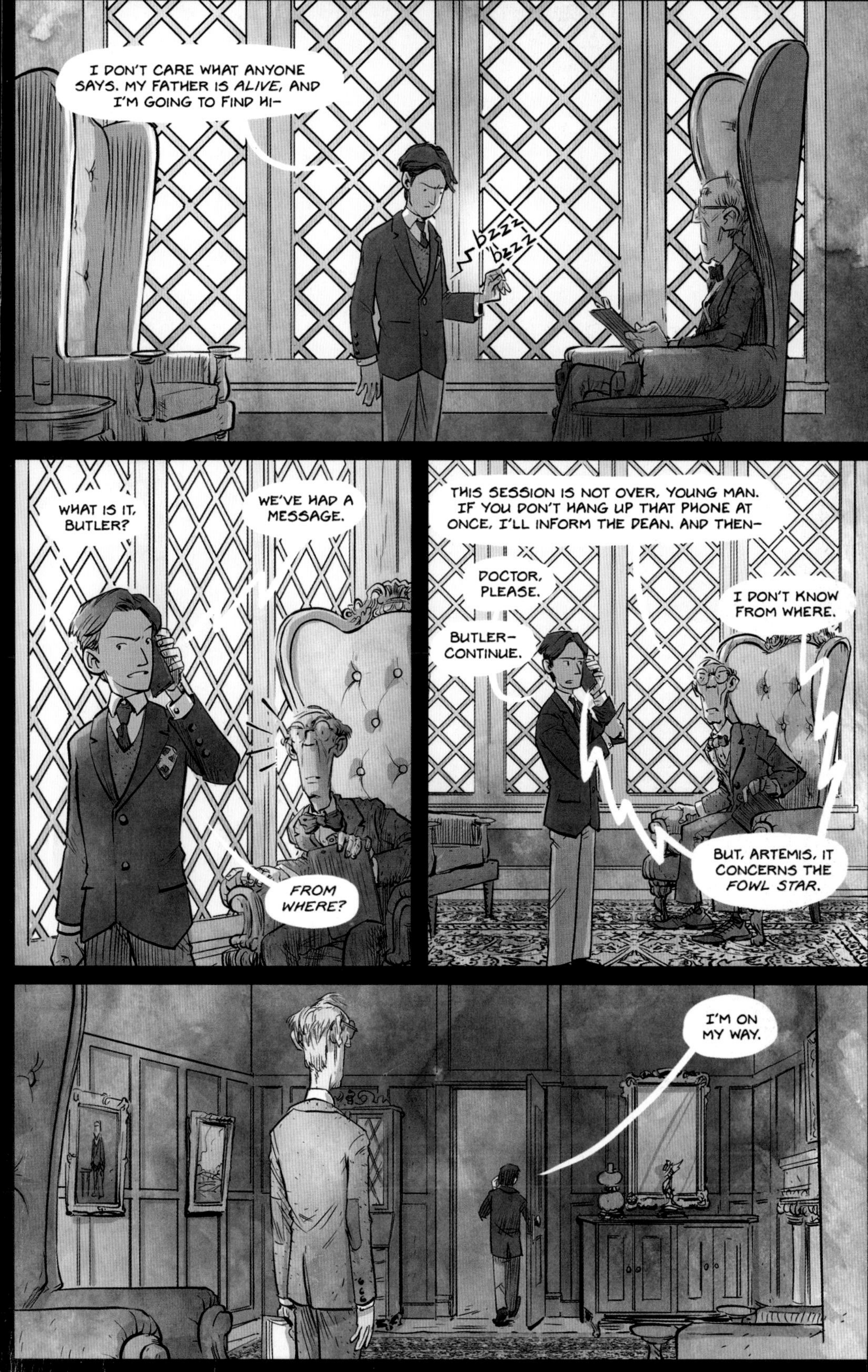
I DON'T CARE WHAT ANYONE SAYS. MY FATHER IS *ALIVE*, AND I'M GOING TO FIND HI–
bzzz bzzz
WHAT IS IT, BUTLER?
WE'VE HAD A MESSAGE.
FROM WHERE?
THIS SESSION IS NOT OVER, YOUNG MAN. IF YOU DON'T HANG UP THAT PHONE AT ONCE, I'LL INFORM THE DEAN. AND THEN–
DOCTOR, PLEASE.
BUTLER– CONTINUE.
I DON'T KNOW FROM WHERE.
BUT, ARTEMIS, IT CONCERNS THE *FOWL STAR*.
I'M ON MY WAY.

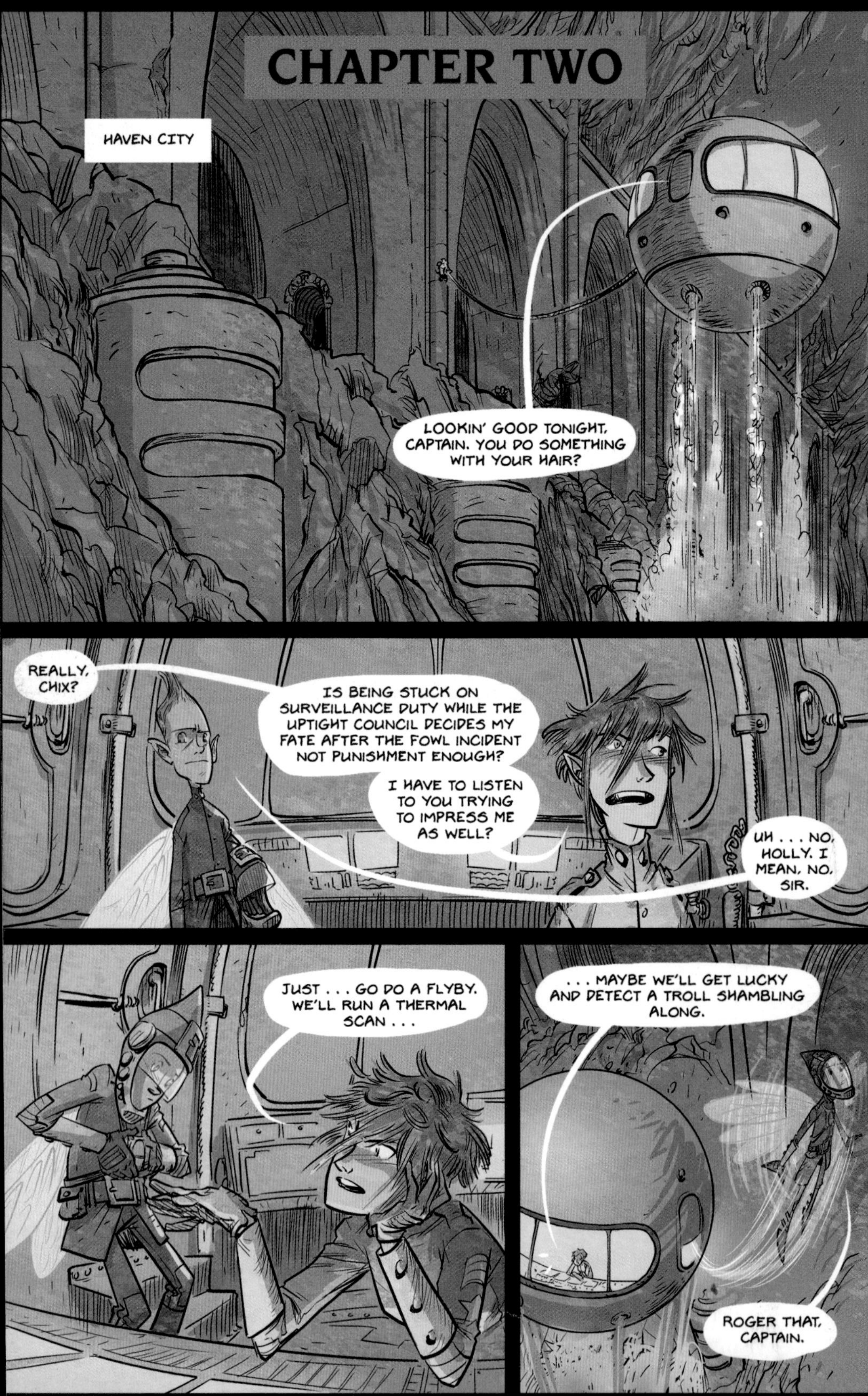
CHAPTER TWO
HAVEN CITY
LOOKIN' GOOD TONIGHT, CAPTAIN. YOU DO SOMETHING WITH YOUR HAIR?
REALLY, CHIX?
IS BEING STUCK ON SURVEILLANCE DUTY WHILE THE UPTIGHT COUNCIL DECIDES MY FATE AFTER THE FOWL INCIDENT NOT PUNISHMENT ENOUGH?
I HAVE TO LISTEN TO YOU TRYING TO IMPRESS ME AS WELL?
UH . . . NO, HOLLY. I MEAN, NO, SIR.
JUST . . . GO DO A FLYBY. WE'LL RUN A THERMAL SCAN . . .
. . . MAYBE WE'LL GET LUCKY AND DETECT A TROLL SHAMBLING ALONG.
ROGER THAT, CAPTAIN.

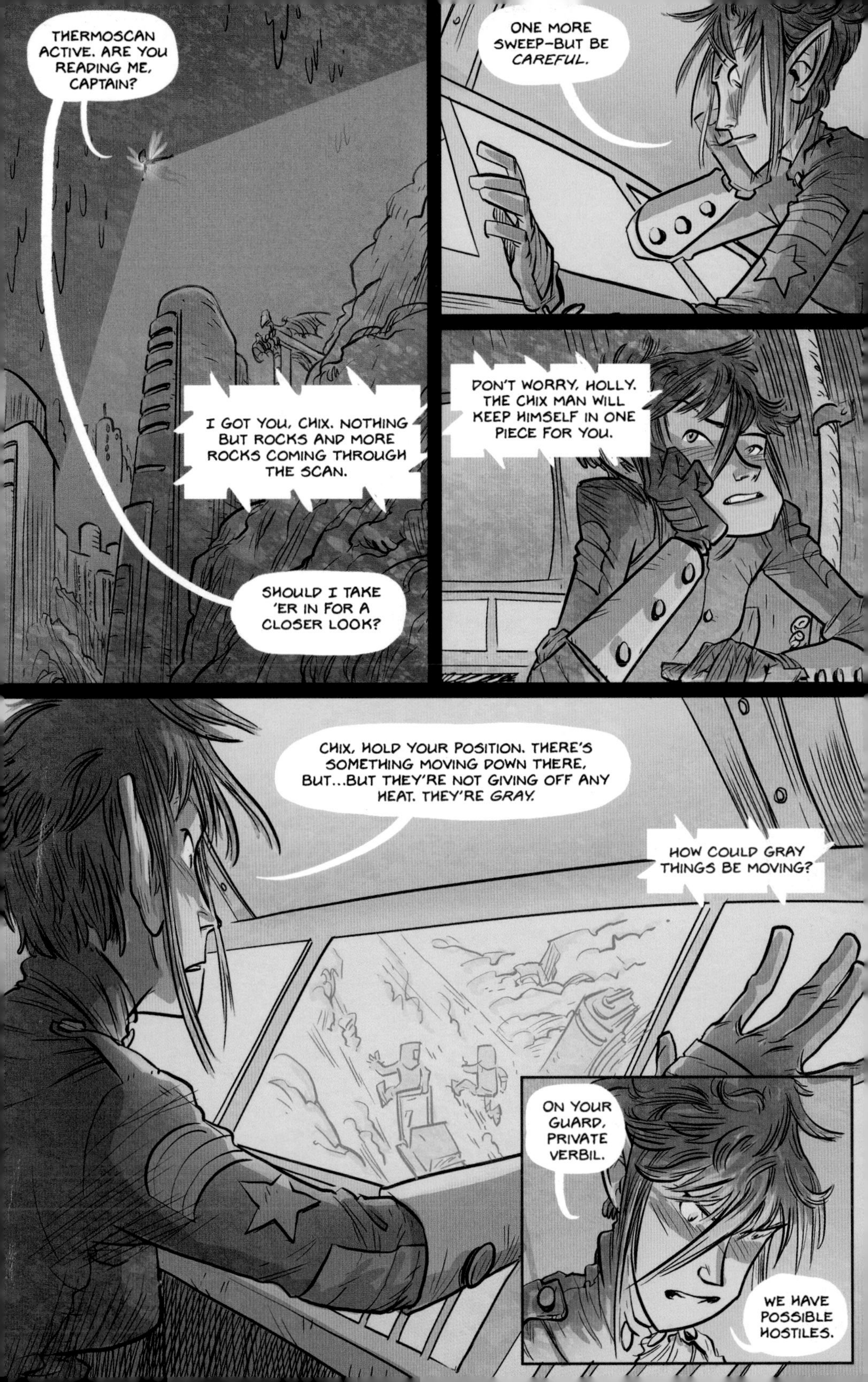
THERMOSCAN ACTIVE. ARE YOU READING ME, CAPTAIN?
I GOT YOU, CHIX. NOTHING BUT ROCKS AND MORE ROCKS COMING THROUGH THE SCAN.
SHOULD I TAKE 'ER IN FOR A CLOSER LOOK?
ONE MORE SWEEP—BUT BE *CAREFUL*.
DON'T WORRY, HOLLY. THE CHIX MAN WILL KEEP HIMSELF IN ONE PIECE FOR YOU.
CHIX, HOLD YOUR POSITION. THERE'S SOMETHING MOVING DOWN THERE, BUT...BUT THEY'RE NOT GIVING OFF ANY HEAT. THEY'RE *GRAY*.
HOW COULD GRAY THINGS BE MOVING?
ON YOUR GUARD, PRIVATE VERBIL.
WE HAVE POSSIBLE HOSTILES.

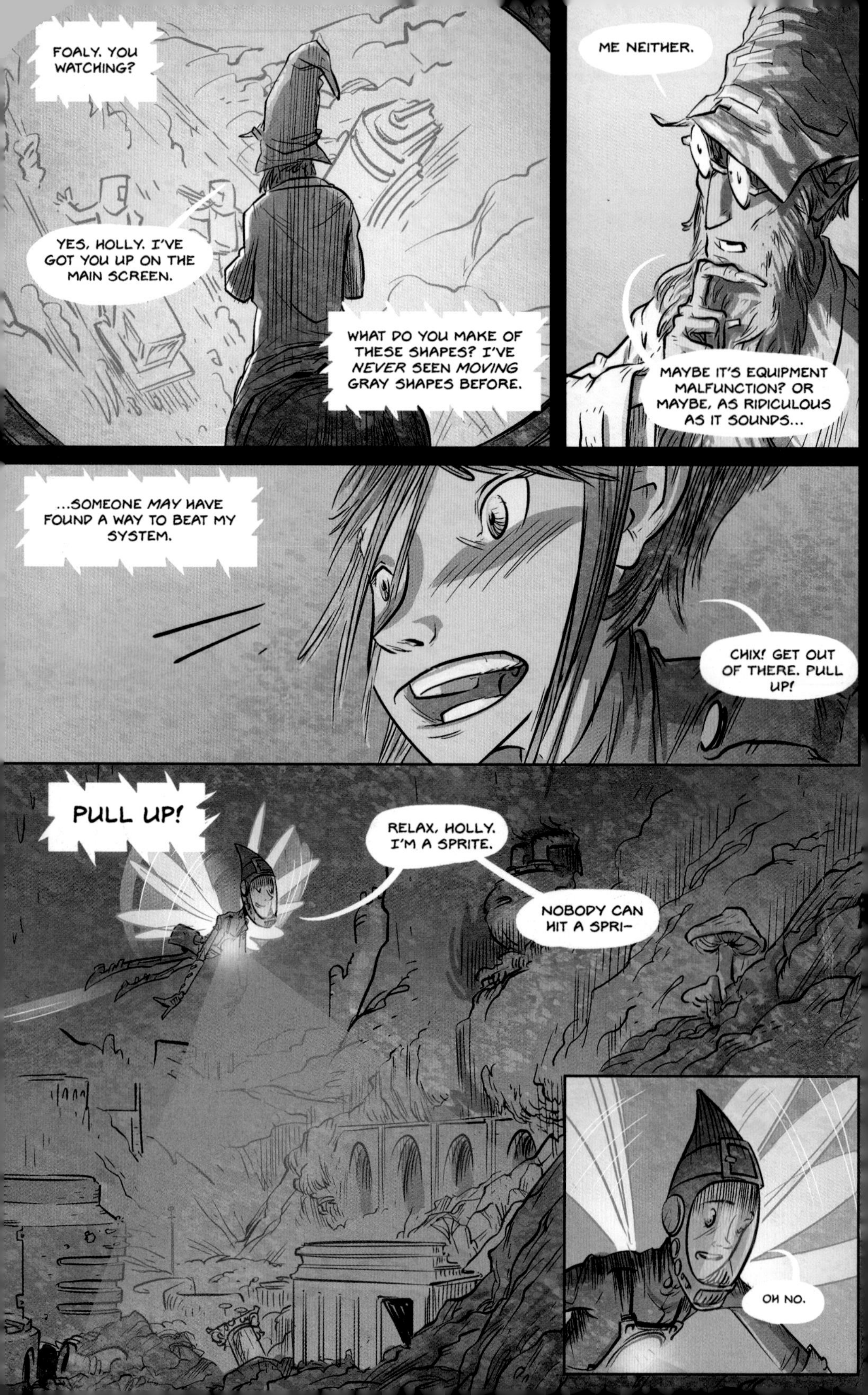
FOALY. YOU WATCHING?
YES, HOLLY. I'VE GOT YOU UP ON THE MAIN SCREEN.
WHAT DO YOU MAKE OF THESE SHAPES? I'VE *NEVER* SEEN *MOVING* GRAY SHAPES BEFORE.
ME NEITHER.
MAYBE IT'S EQUIPMENT MALFUNCTION? OR MAYBE, AS RIDICULOUS AS IT SOUNDS...
...SOMEONE *MAY* HAVE FOUND A WAY TO BEAT MY SYSTEM.
CHIX! GET OUT OF THERE. PULL UP!
PULL UP!
RELAX, HOLLY. I'M A SPRITE.
NOBODY CAN HIT A SPRI–
OH NO.

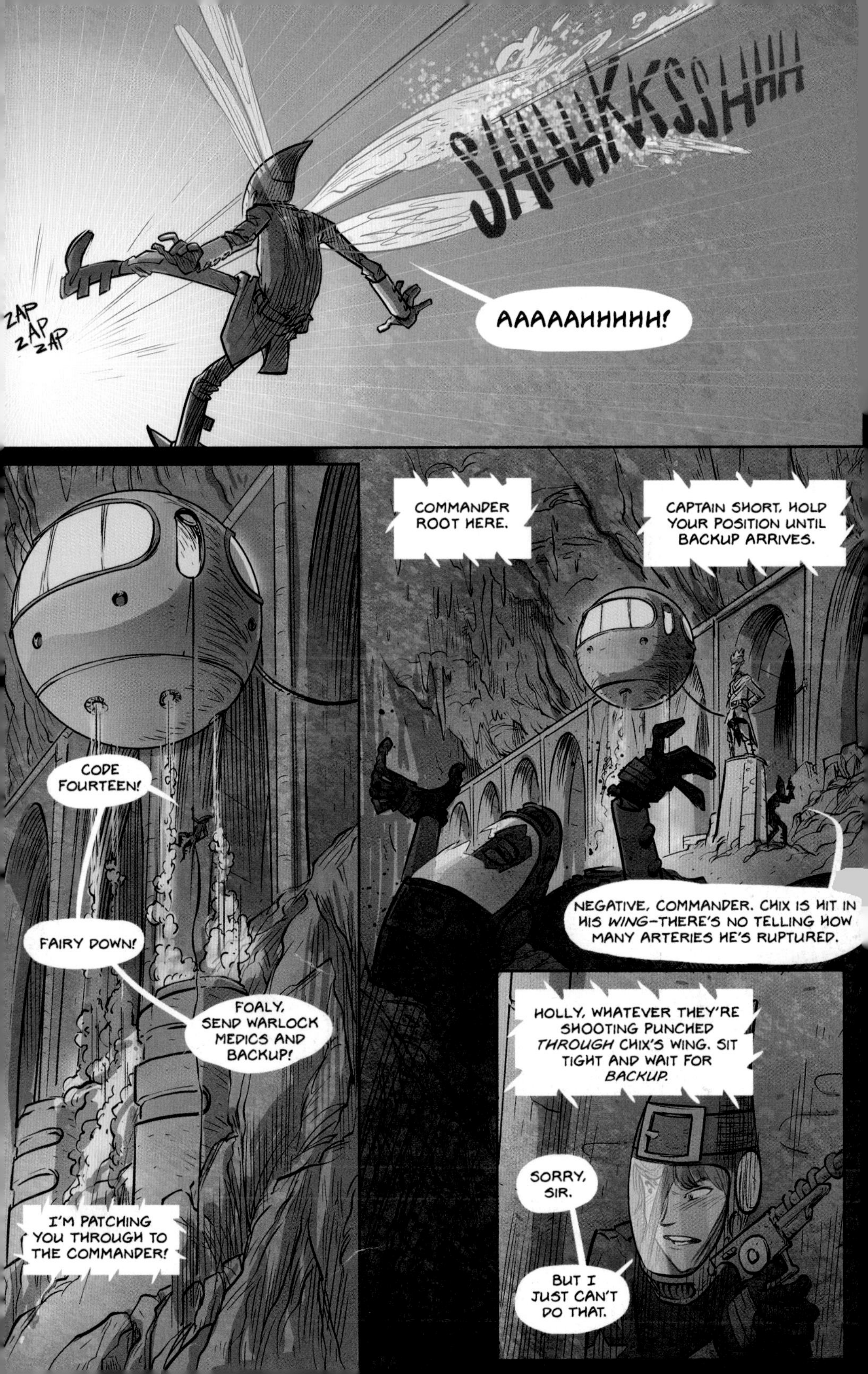
SHHHKKSSHHHH
ZAP ZAP ZAP
AAAAAHHHHH!
CODE FOURTEEN!
FAIRY DOWN!
FOALY, SEND WARLOCK MEDICS AND BACKUP!
I'M PATCHING YOU THROUGH TO THE COMMANDER!
COMMANDER ROOT HERE.
CAPTAIN SHORT, HOLD YOUR POSITION UNTIL BACKUP ARRIVES.
NEGATIVE, COMMANDER. CHIX IS HIT IN HIS *WING*—THERE'S NO TELLING HOW MANY ARTERIES HE'S RUPTURED.
HOLLY, WHATEVER THEY'RE SHOOTING PUNCHED *THROUGH* CHIX'S WING. SIT TIGHT AND WAIT FOR *BACKUP.*
SORRY, SIR.
BUT I JUST CAN'T DO THAT.

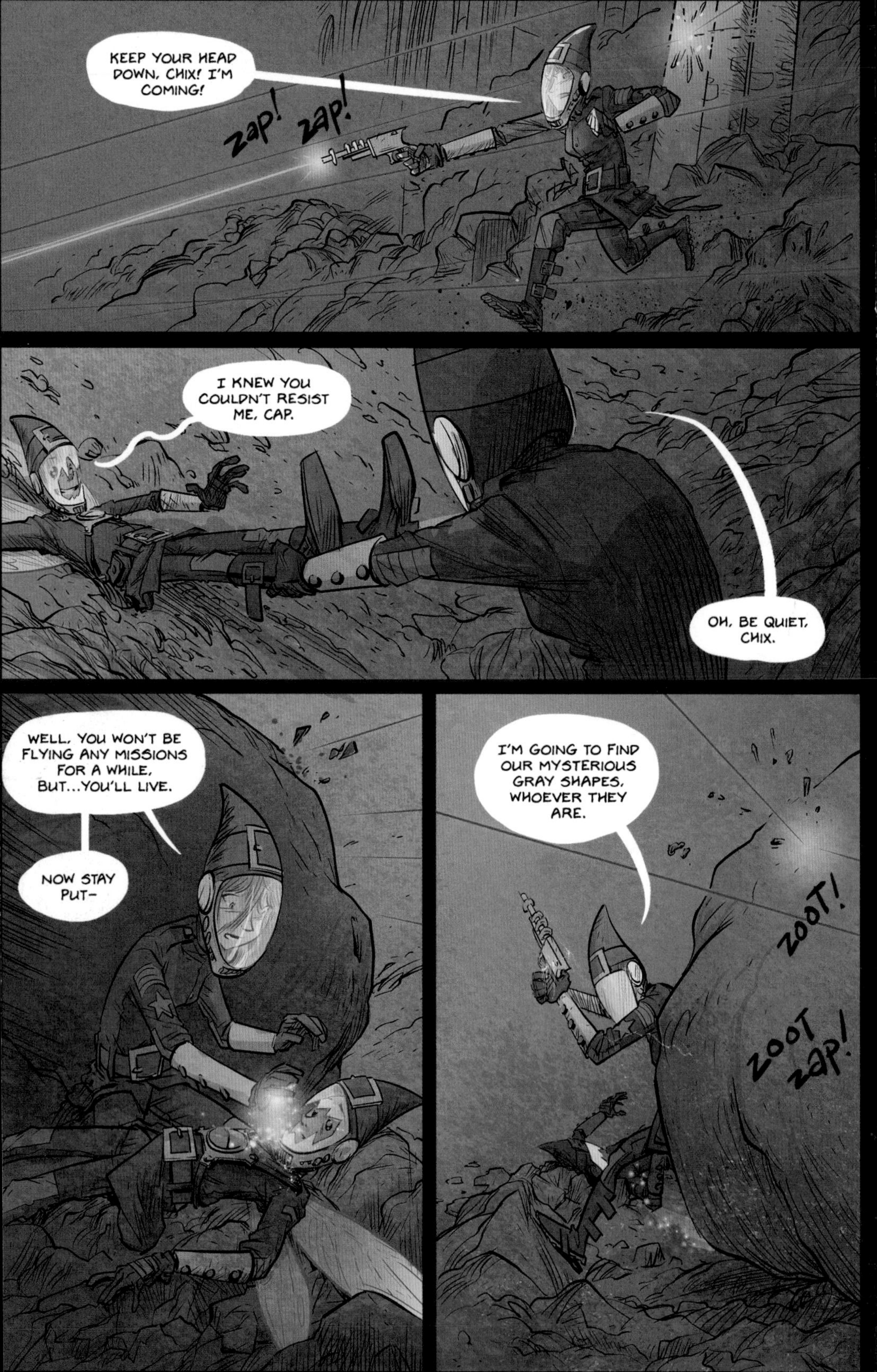
KEEP YOUR HEAD DOWN, CHIX! I'M COMING!
ZAP! ZAP!
I KNEW YOU COULDN'T RESIST ME, CAP.
OH, BE QUIET, CHIX.
WELL, YOU WON'T BE FLYING ANY MISSIONS FOR A WHILE, BUT...YOU'LL LIVE.
NOW STAY PUT-
I'M GOING TO FIND OUR MYSTERIOUS GRAY SHAPES, WHOEVER THEY ARE.
ZOOT!
ZOOT ZAP!

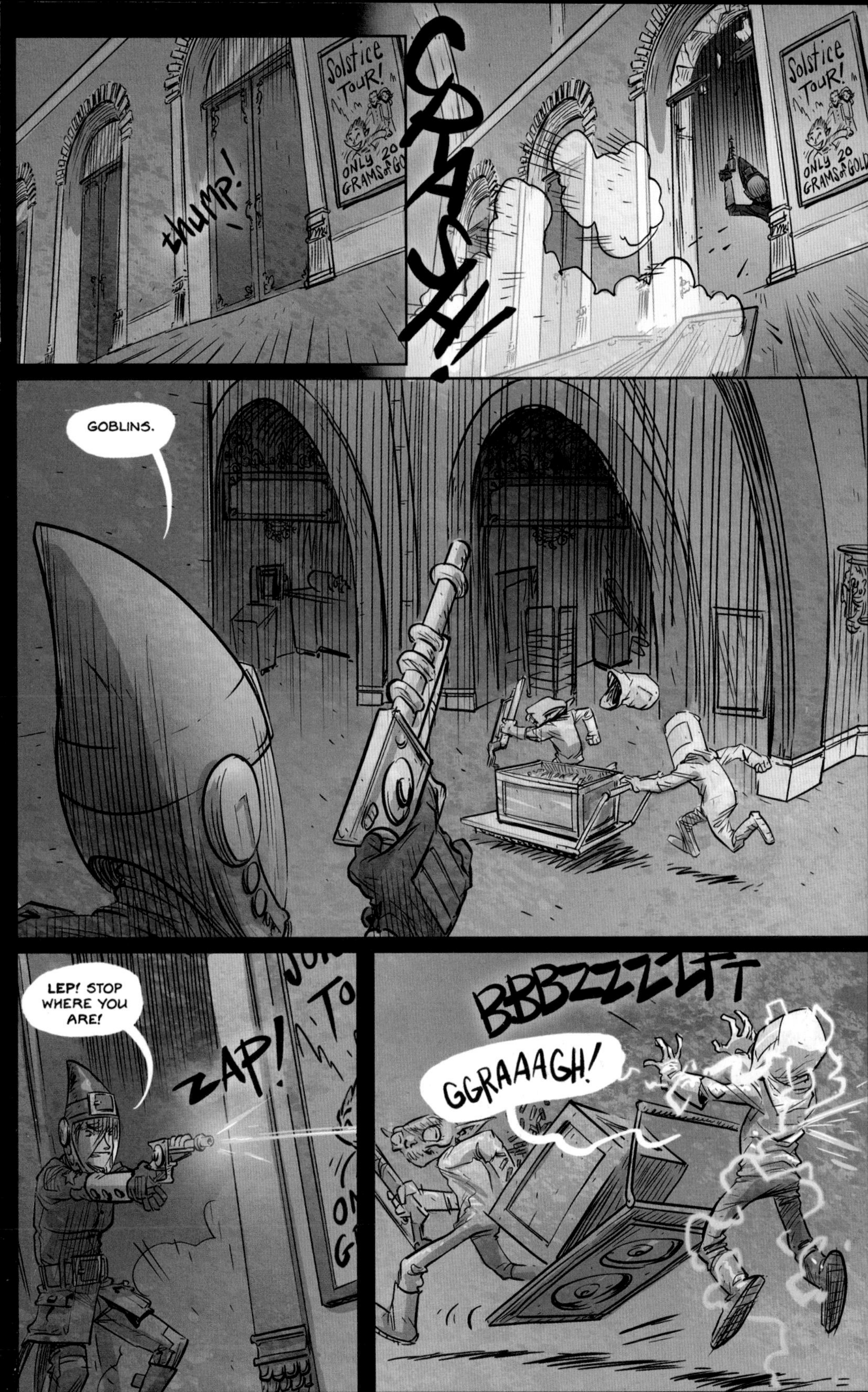
Solstice TOUR!
ONLY 20 GRAMS of GOLD
thump!
CRASH!
GOBLINS.
LEP! STOP WHERE YOU ARE!
ZAP!
BBBZZZZZZTT
GGRAAAGH!

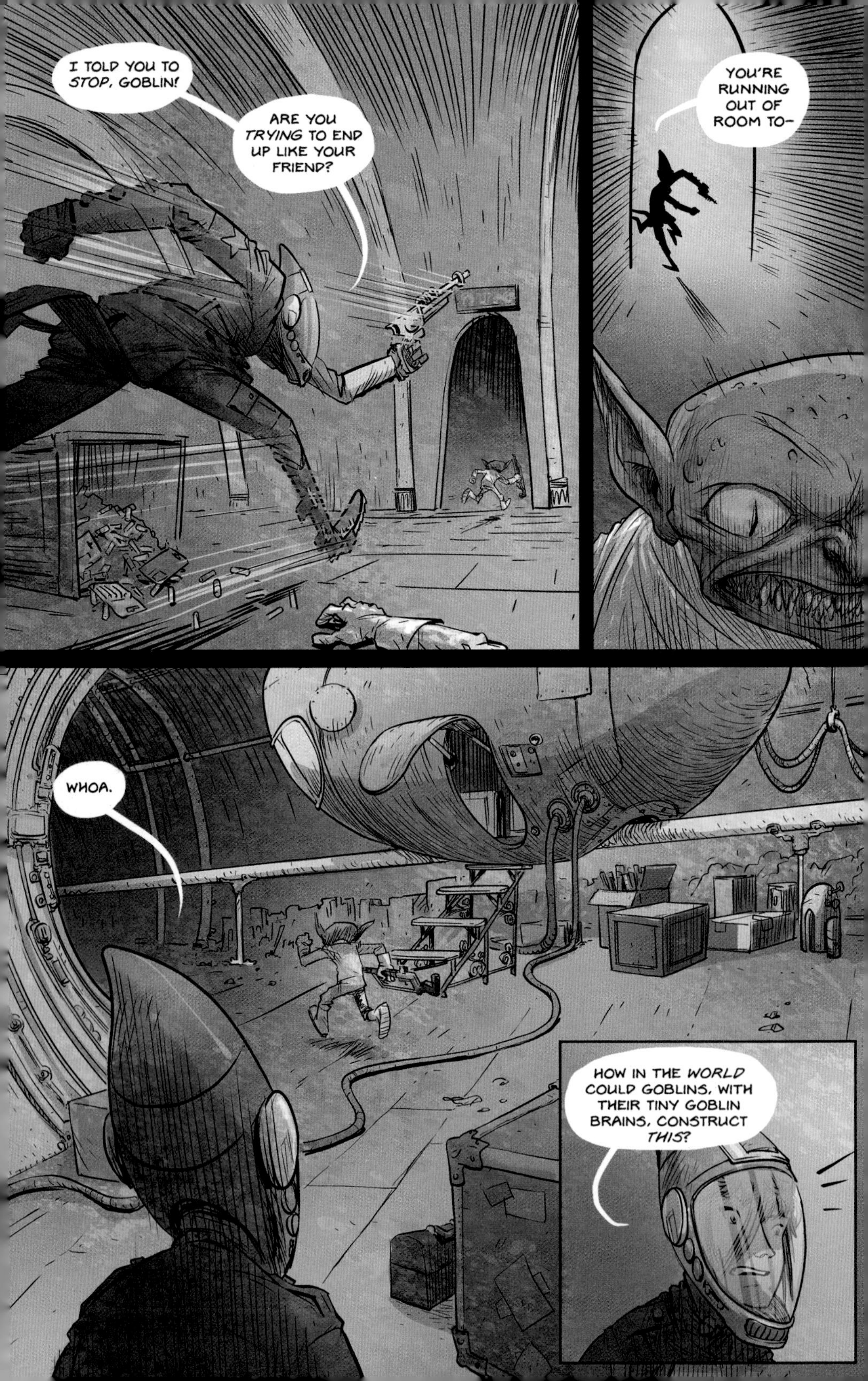
I TOLD YOU TO *STOP*, GOBLIN!
ARE YOU *TRYING* TO END UP LIKE YOUR FRIEND?
YOU'RE RUNNING OUT OF ROOM TO-
WHOA.
HOW IN THE *WORLD* COULD GOBLINS, WITH THEIR TINY GOBLIN BRAINS, CONSTRUCT *THIS*?

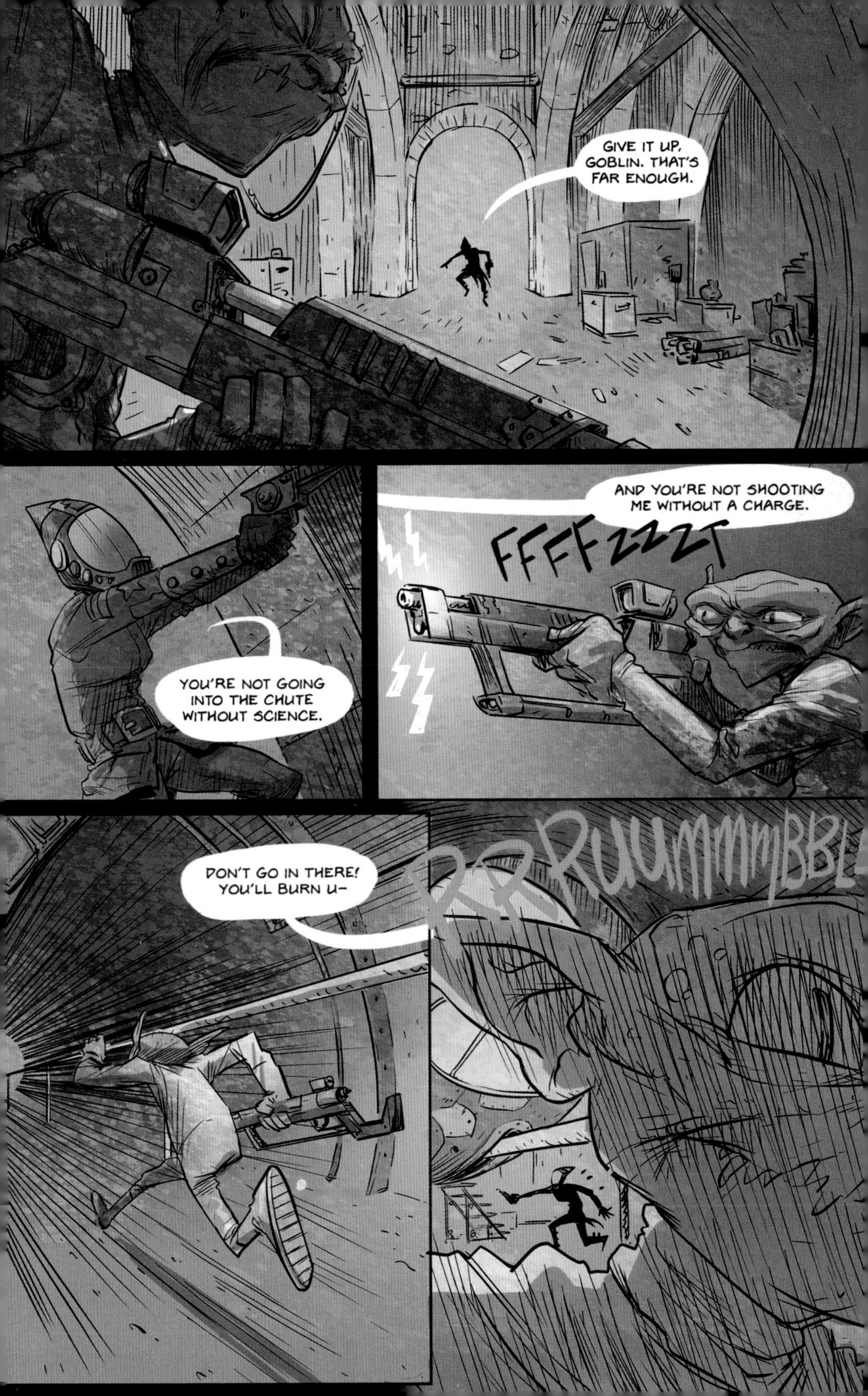
GIVE IT UP, GOBLIN. THAT'S FAR ENOUGH.
YOU'RE NOT GOING INTO THE CHUTE WITHOUT SCIENCE.
AND YOU'RE NOT SHOOTING ME WITHOUT A CHARGE.
FFFFZZZT
DON'T GO IN THERE! YOU'LL BURN U–
RRRUUMMMBBL

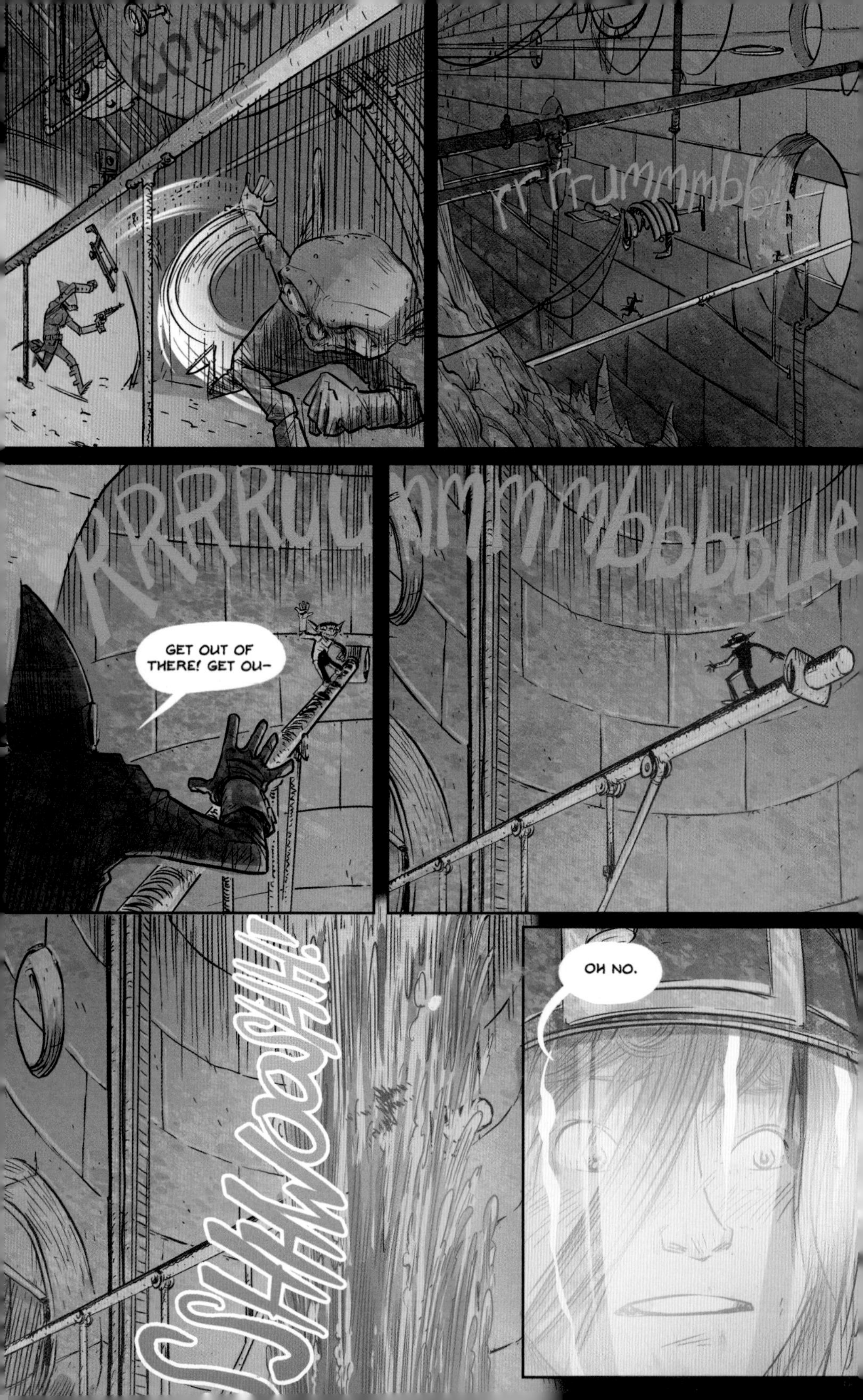
rrrrummmbbl
RRRRUUMMMMBBBLLE
GET OUT OF THERE! GET OU-
SHHWOOSH!!
OH NO.

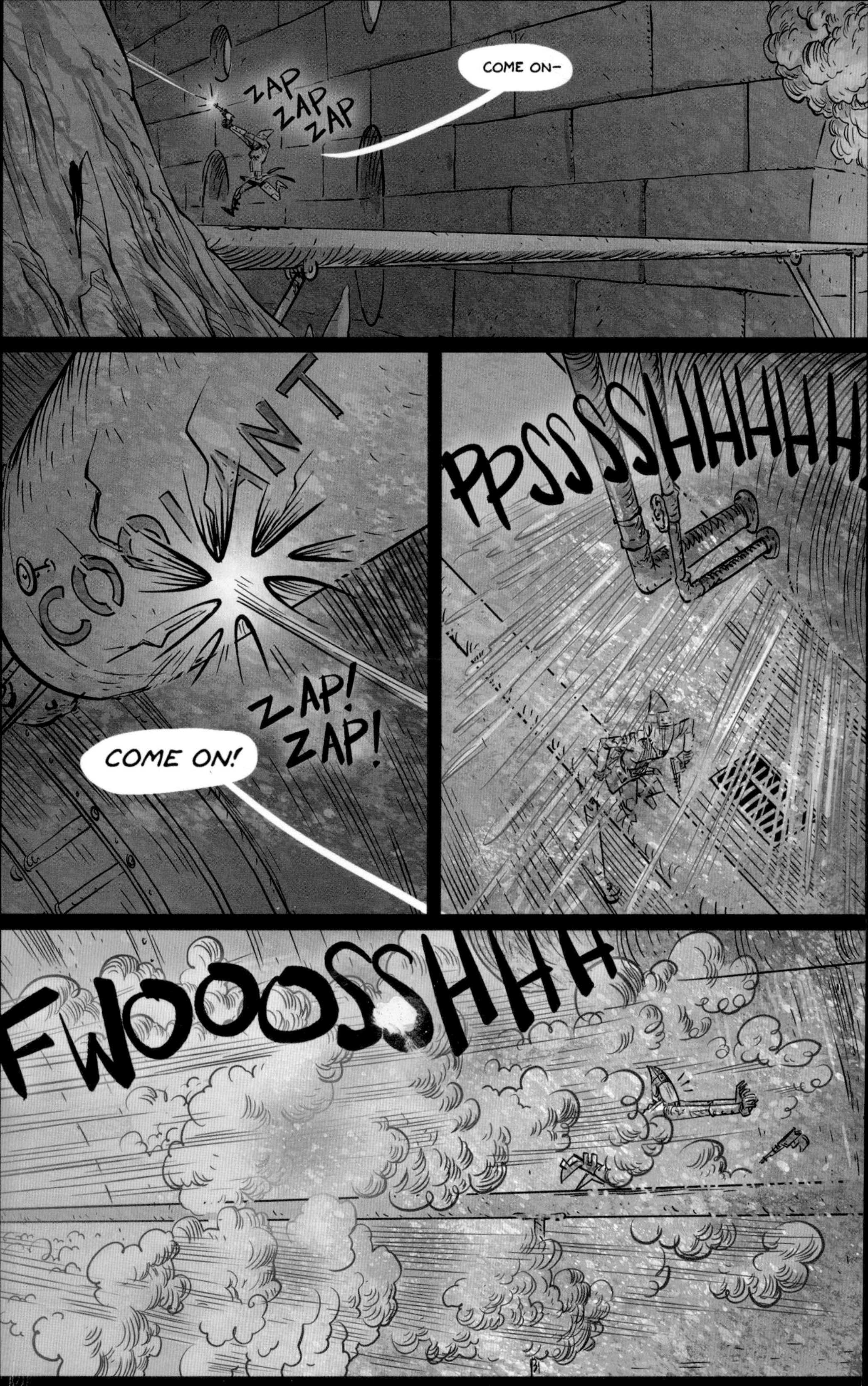

ZAP
ZAP
ZAP
COME ON–
ZAP!
ZAP!
COME ON!
PPSSSSHHHHH
FWOOOSSHHH

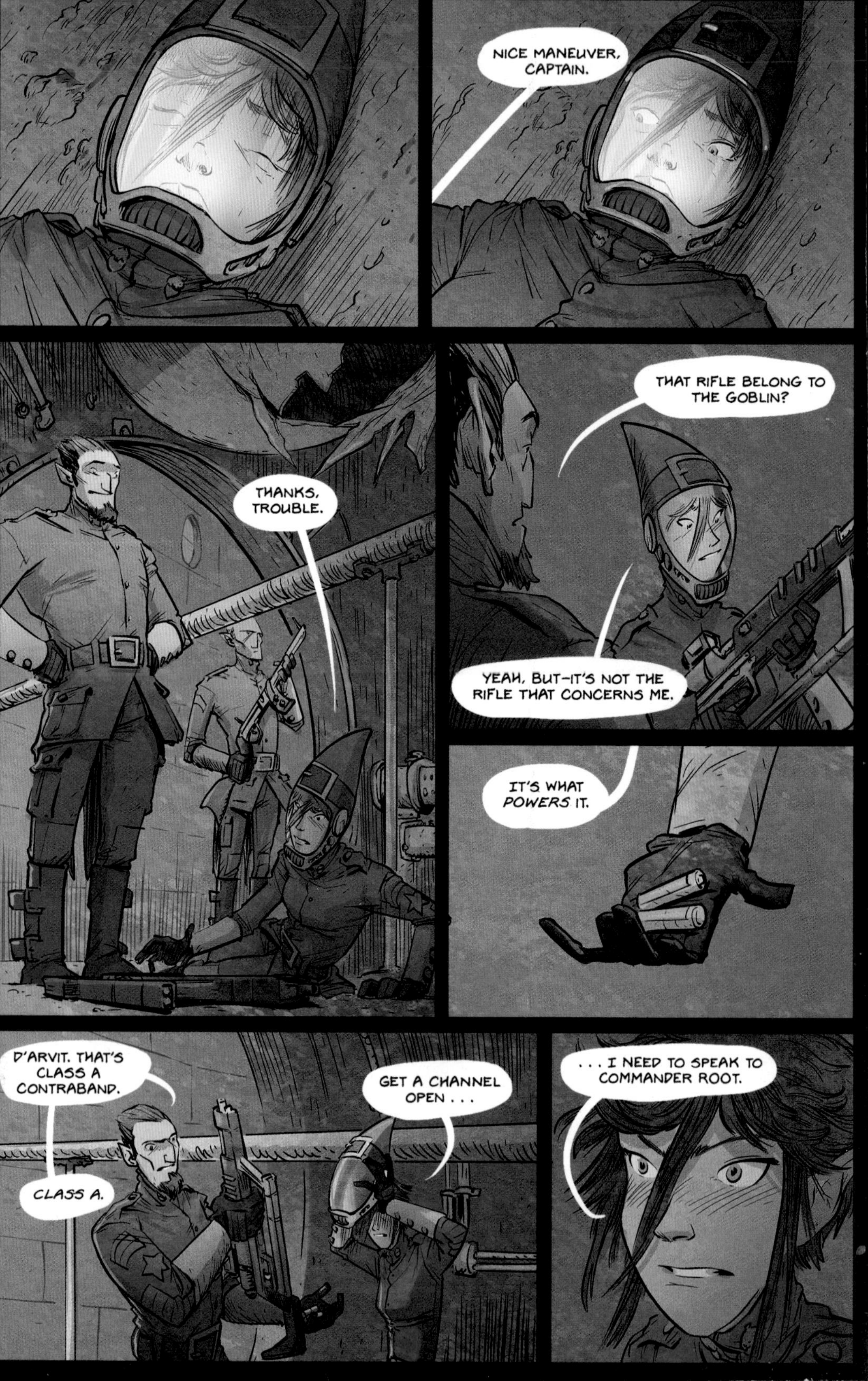
NICE MANEUVER, CAPTAIN.
THANKS, TROUBLE.
THAT RIFLE BELONG TO THE GOBLIN?
YEAH, BUT—IT'S NOT THE RIFLE THAT CONCERNS ME.
IT'S WHAT *POWERS* IT.
D'ARVIT. THAT'S CLASS A CONTRABAND.
CLASS A.
GET A CHANNEL OPEN . . .
. . . I NEED TO SPEAK TO COMMANDER ROOT.

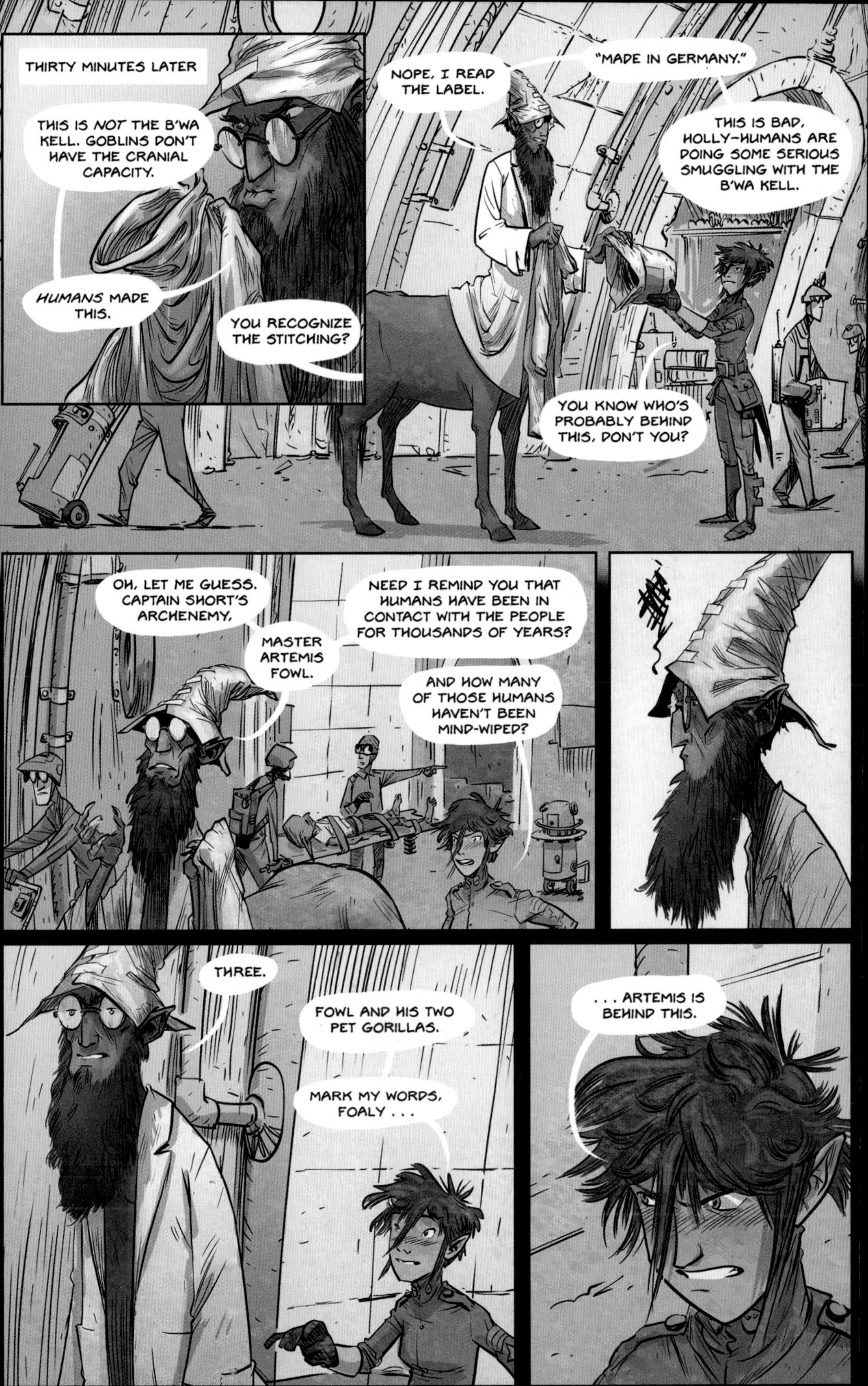
THIRTY MINUTES LATER
THIS IS *NOT* THE B'WA KELL. GOBLINS DON'T HAVE THE CRANIAL CAPACITY.
HUMANS MADE THIS.
YOU RECOGNIZE THE STITCHING?
NOPE, I READ THE LABEL.
"MADE IN GERMANY."
THIS IS BAD, HOLLY—HUMANS ARE DOING SOME SERIOUS SMUGGLING WITH THE B'WA KELL.
YOU KNOW WHO'S PROBABLY BEHIND THIS, DON'T YOU?
OH, LET ME GUESS. CAPTAIN SHORT'S ARCHENEMY,
MASTER ARTEMIS FOWL.
NEED I REMIND YOU THAT HUMANS HAVE BEEN IN CONTACT WITH THE PEOPLE FOR THOUSANDS OF YEARS?
AND HOW MANY OF THOSE HUMANS HAVEN'T BEEN MIND-WIPED?
THREE.
FOWL AND HIS TWO PET GORILLAS.
MARK MY WORDS, FOALY . . .
. . . ARTEMIS IS BEHIND THIS.

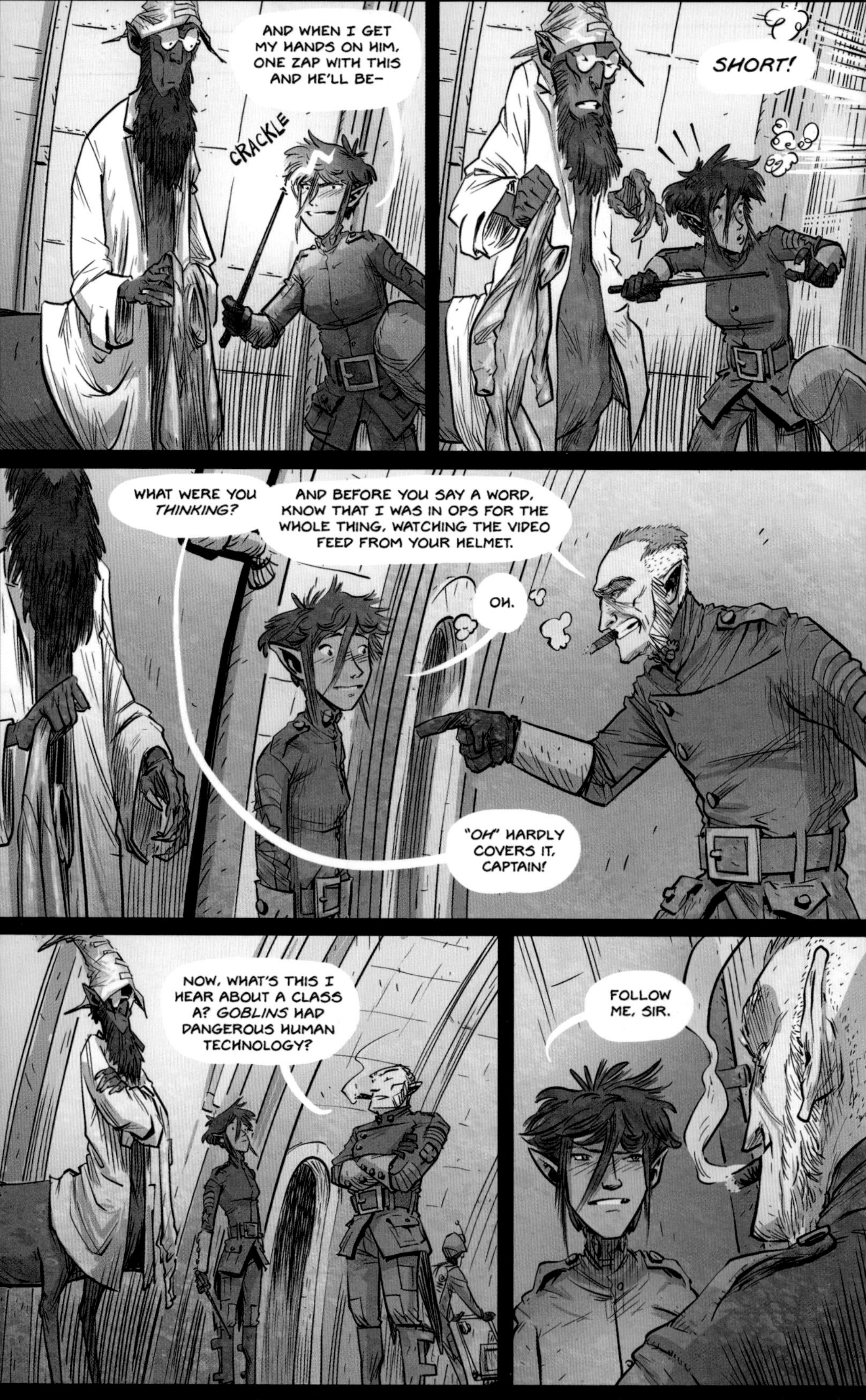
AND WHEN I GET MY HANDS ON HIM, ONE ZAP WITH THIS AND HE'LL BE—
CRACKLE
SHORT!
WHAT WERE YOU *THINKING?*
AND BEFORE YOU SAY A WORD, KNOW THAT I WAS IN OPS FOR THE WHOLE THING, WATCHING THE VIDEO FEED FROM YOUR HELMET.
OH.
"*OH*" HARDLY COVERS IT, CAPTAIN!
NOW, WHAT'S THIS I HEAR ABOUT A CLASS A? *GOBLINS* HAD DANGEROUS HUMAN TECHNOLOGY?
FOLLOW ME, SIR.

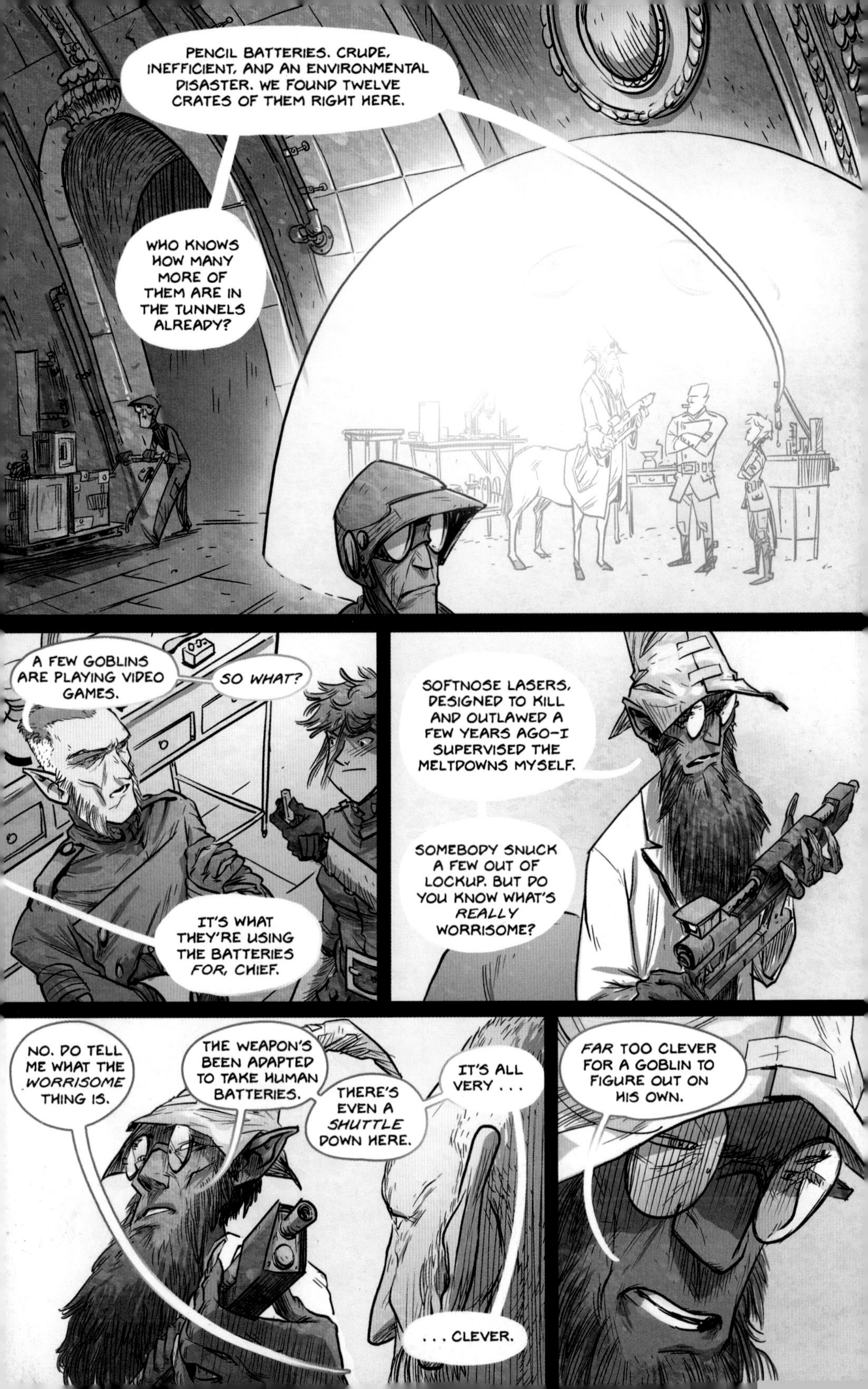
PENCIL BATTERIES. CRUDE, INEFFICIENT, AND AN ENVIRONMENTAL DISASTER. WE FOUND TWELVE CRATES OF THEM RIGHT HERE.
WHO KNOWS HOW MANY MORE OF THEM ARE IN THE TUNNELS ALREADY?
A FEW GOBLINS ARE PLAYING VIDEO GAMES.
SO WHAT?
IT'S WHAT THEY'RE USING THE BATTERIES FOR, CHIEF.
SOFTNOSE LASERS, DESIGNED TO KILL AND OUTLAWED A FEW YEARS AGO—I SUPERVISED THE MELTDOWNS MYSELF.
SOMEBODY SNUCK A FEW OUT OF LOCKUP. BUT DO YOU KNOW WHAT'S REALLY WORRISOME?
NO. DO TELL ME WHAT THE WORRISOME THING IS.
THE WEAPON'S BEEN ADAPTED TO TAKE HUMAN BATTERIES.
THERE'S EVEN A SHUTTLE DOWN HERE.
IT'S ALL VERY . . .
. . . CLEVER.
FAR TOO CLEVER FOR A GOBLIN TO FIGURE OUT ON HIS OWN.

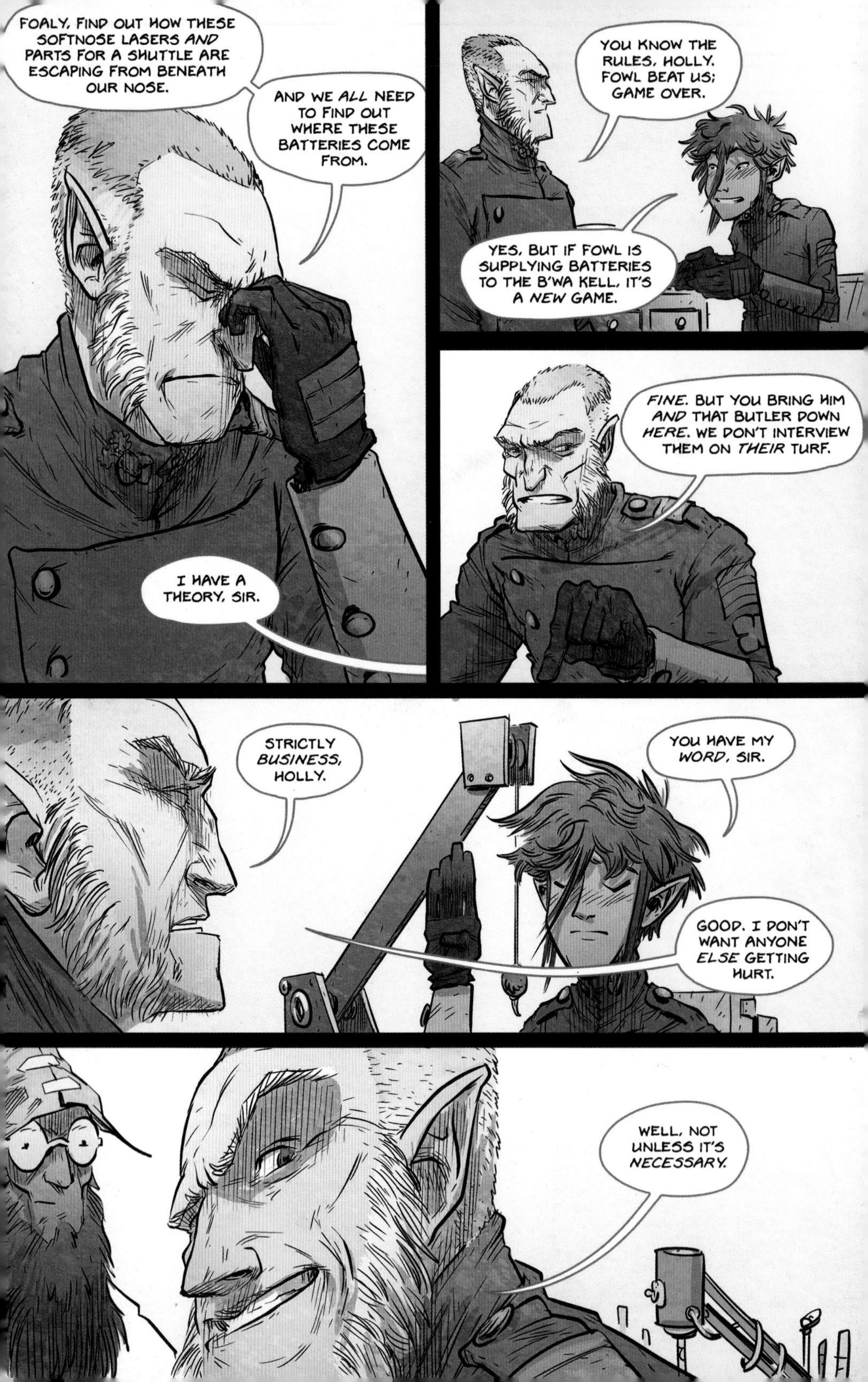
FOALY, FIND OUT HOW THESE SOFTNOSE LASERS *AND* PARTS FOR A SHUTTLE ARE ESCAPING FROM BENEATH OUR NOSE.
AND WE *ALL* NEED TO FIND OUT WHERE THESE BATTERIES COME FROM.
I HAVE A THEORY, SIR.
YOU KNOW THE RULES, HOLLY. FOWL BEAT US; GAME OVER.
YES, BUT IF FOWL IS SUPPLYING BATTERIES TO THE B'WA KELL, IT'S A *NEW* GAME.
FINE. BUT YOU BRING HIM *AND* THAT BUTLER DOWN *HERE*. WE DON'T INTERVIEW THEM ON *THEIR* TURF.
STRICTLY *BUSINESS*, HOLLY.
YOU HAVE MY *WORD*, SIR.
GOOD. I DON'T WANT ANYONE *ELSE* GETTING HURT.
WELL, NOT UNLESS IT'S *NECESSARY*.

CHAPTER THREE

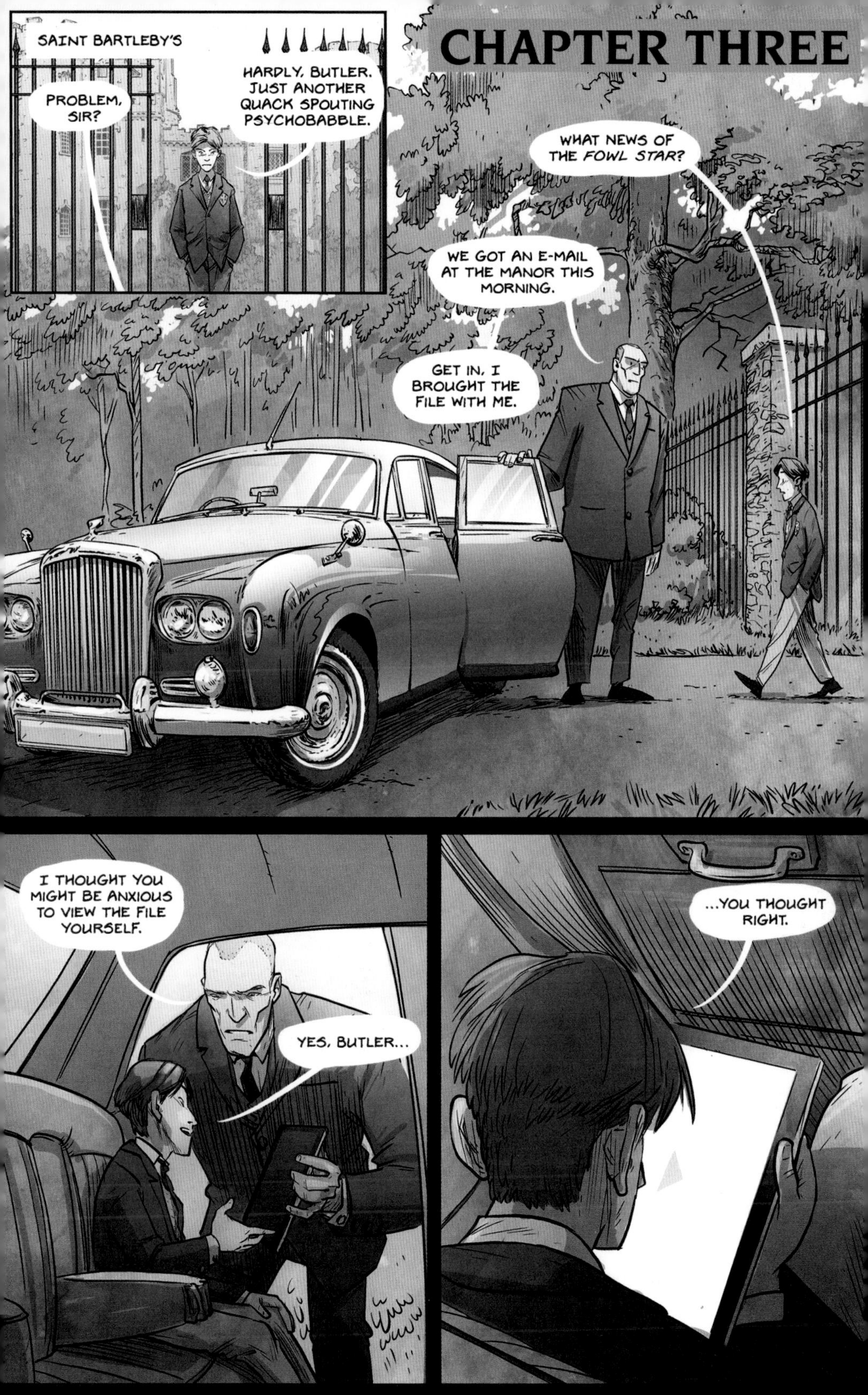
SAINT BARTLEBY'S
PROBLEM, SIR?
HARDLY, BUTLER. JUST ANOTHER QUACK SPOUTING PSYCHOBABBLE.
WHAT NEWS OF THE *FOWL STAR*?
WE GOT AN E-MAIL AT THE MANOR THIS MORNING.
GET IN, I BROUGHT THE FILE WITH ME.
I THOUGHT YOU MIGHT BE ANXIOUS TO VIEW THE FILE YOURSELF.
YES, BUTLER...
...YOU THOUGHT RIGHT.

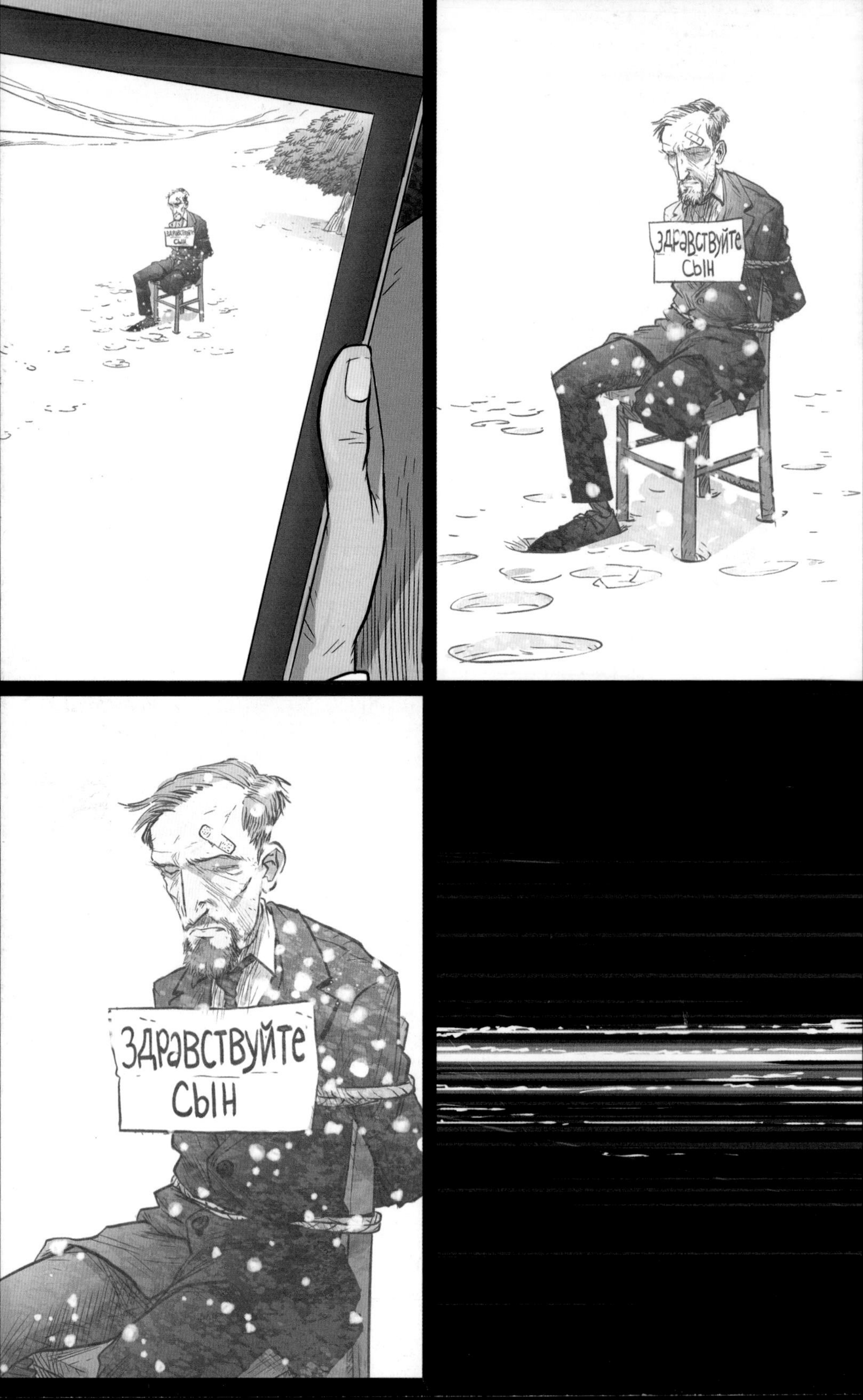
ЗДРАВСТВУЙТЕ
СЫН
ЗДРАВСТВУЙТЕ
СЫН

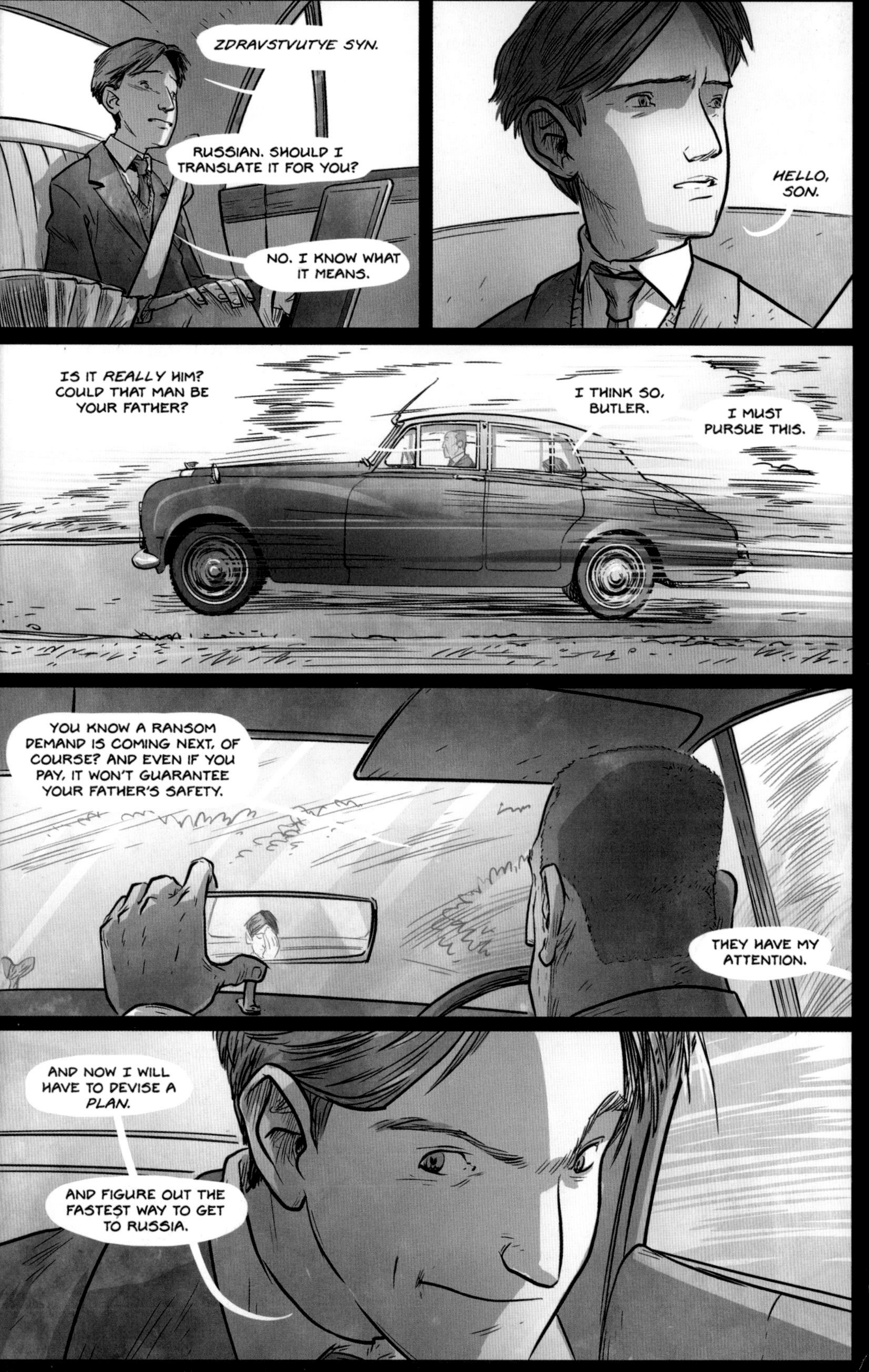
ZDRAVSTVUTYE SYN.
RUSSIAN. SHOULD I TRANSLATE IT FOR YOU?
NO. I KNOW WHAT IT MEANS.
HELLO, SON.
IS IT REALLY HIM? COULD THAT MAN BE YOUR FATHER?
I THINK SO, BUTLER.
I MUST PURSUE THIS.
YOU KNOW A RANSOM DEMAND IS COMING NEXT, OF COURSE? AND EVEN IF YOU PAY, IT WON'T GUARANTEE YOUR FATHER'S SAFETY.
THEY HAVE MY ATTENTION.
AND NOW I WILL HAVE TO DEVISE A PLAN.
AND FIGURE OUT THE FASTEST WAY TO GET TO RUSSIA.

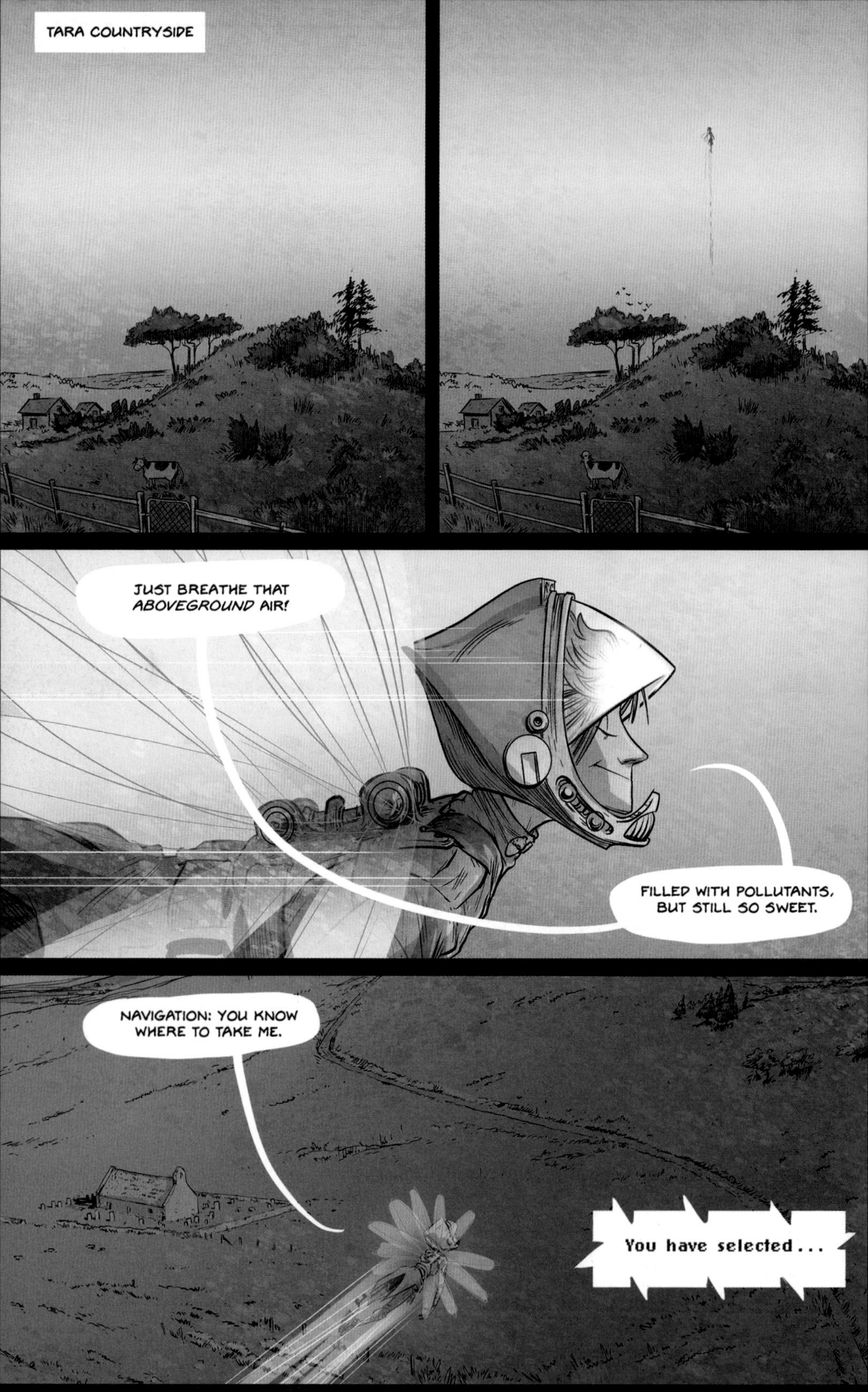
TARA COUNTRYSIDE
JUST BREATHE THAT ABOVEGROUND AIR!
FILLED WITH POLLUTANTS, BUT STILL SO SWEET.
NAVIGATION: YOU KNOW WHERE TO TAKE ME.
You have selected...

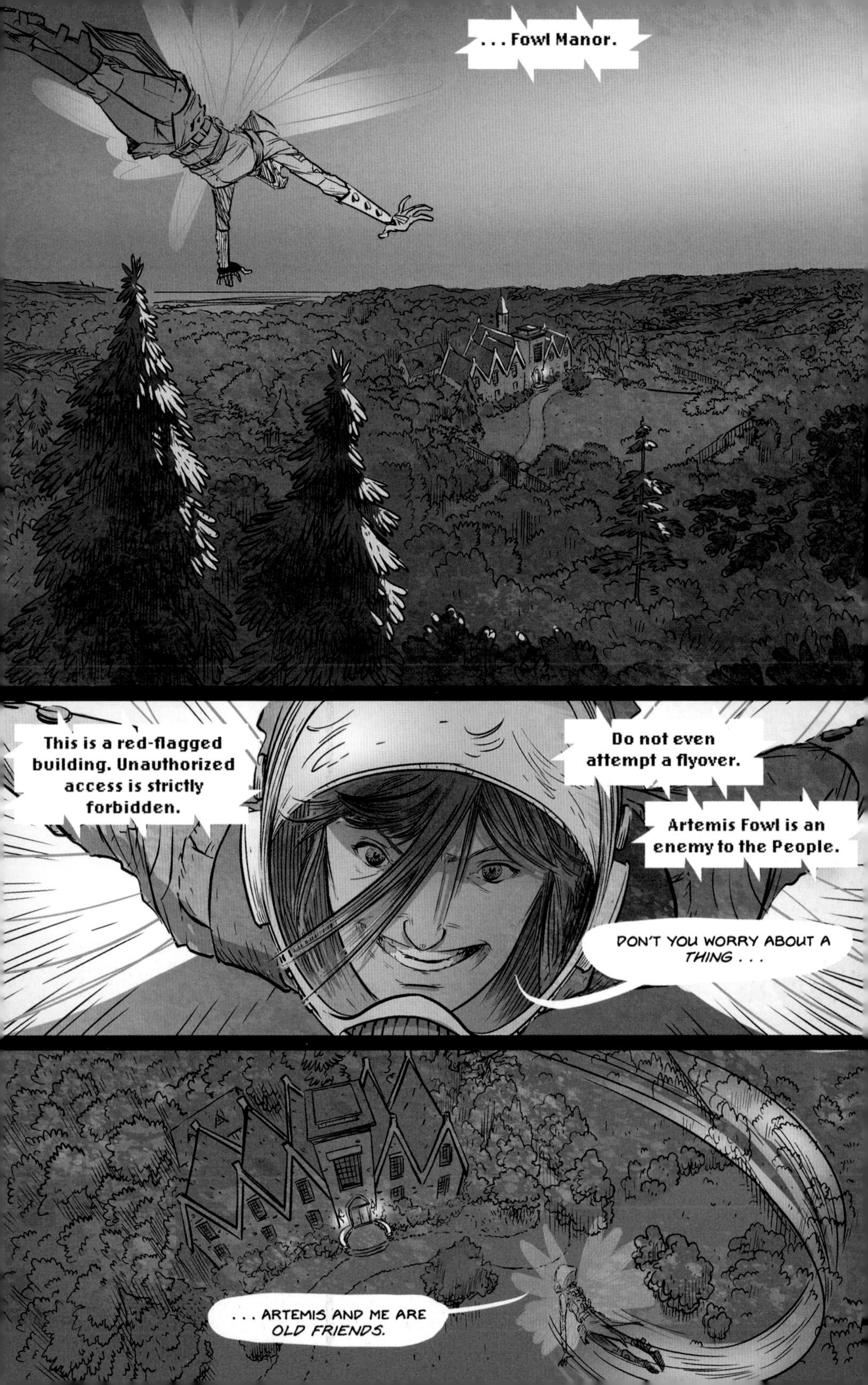
. . . Fowl Manor.
This is a red-flagged building. Unauthorized access is strictly forbidden.
Do not even attempt a flyover.
Artemis Fowl is an enemy to the People.
DON'T YOU WORRY ABOUT A *THING* . . .
. . . ARTEMIS AND ME ARE *OLD FRIENDS*.

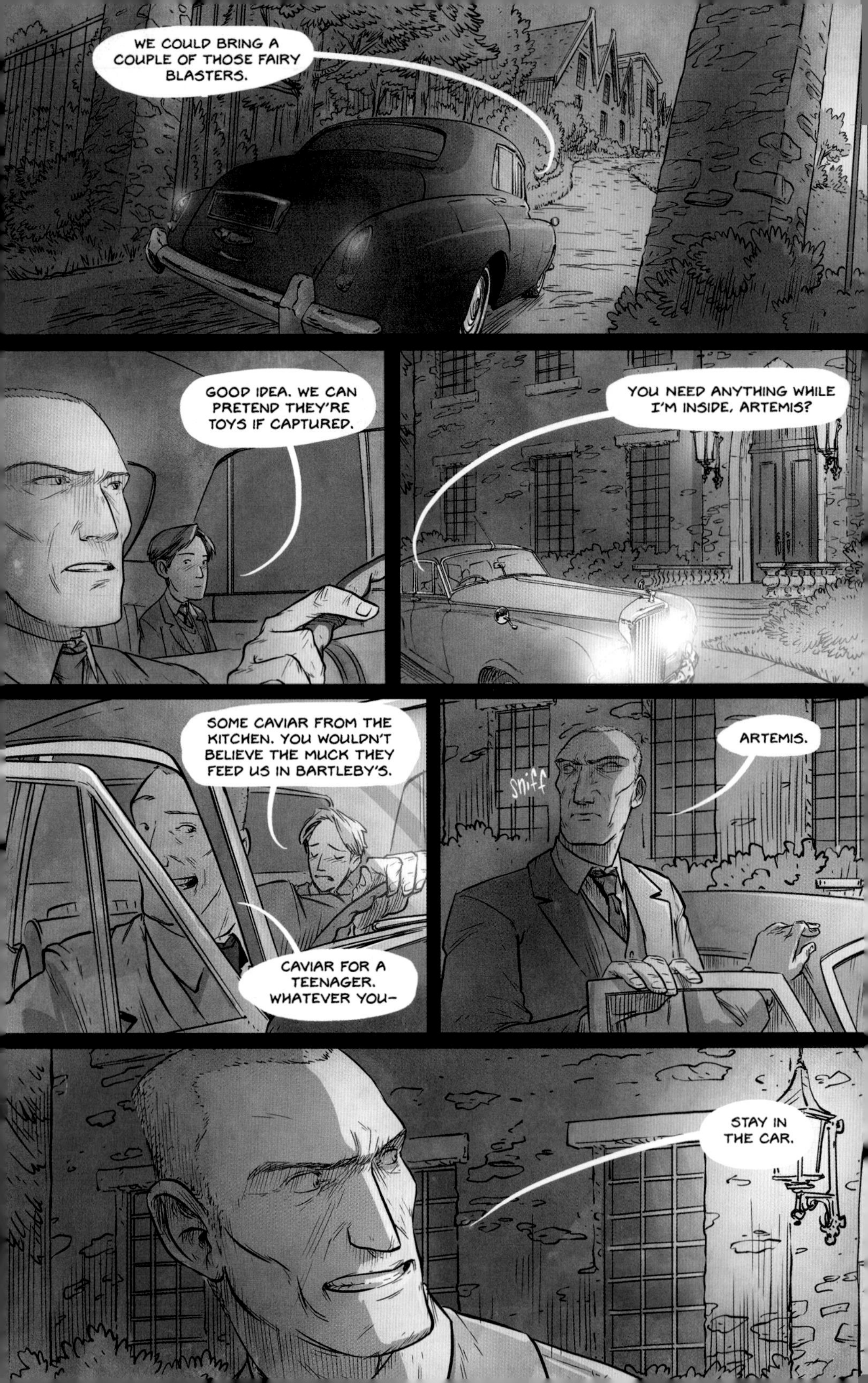
WE COULD BRING A COUPLE OF THOSE FAIRY BLASTERS.
GOOD IDEA. WE CAN PRETEND THEY'RE TOYS IF CAPTURED.
YOU NEED ANYTHING WHILE I'M INSIDE, ARTEMIS?
SOME CAVIAR FROM THE KITCHEN. YOU WOULDN'T BELIEVE THE MUCK THEY FEED US IN BARTLEBY'S.
CAVIAR FOR A TEENAGER. WHATEVER YOU-
sniff
ARTEMIS.
STAY IN THE CAR.

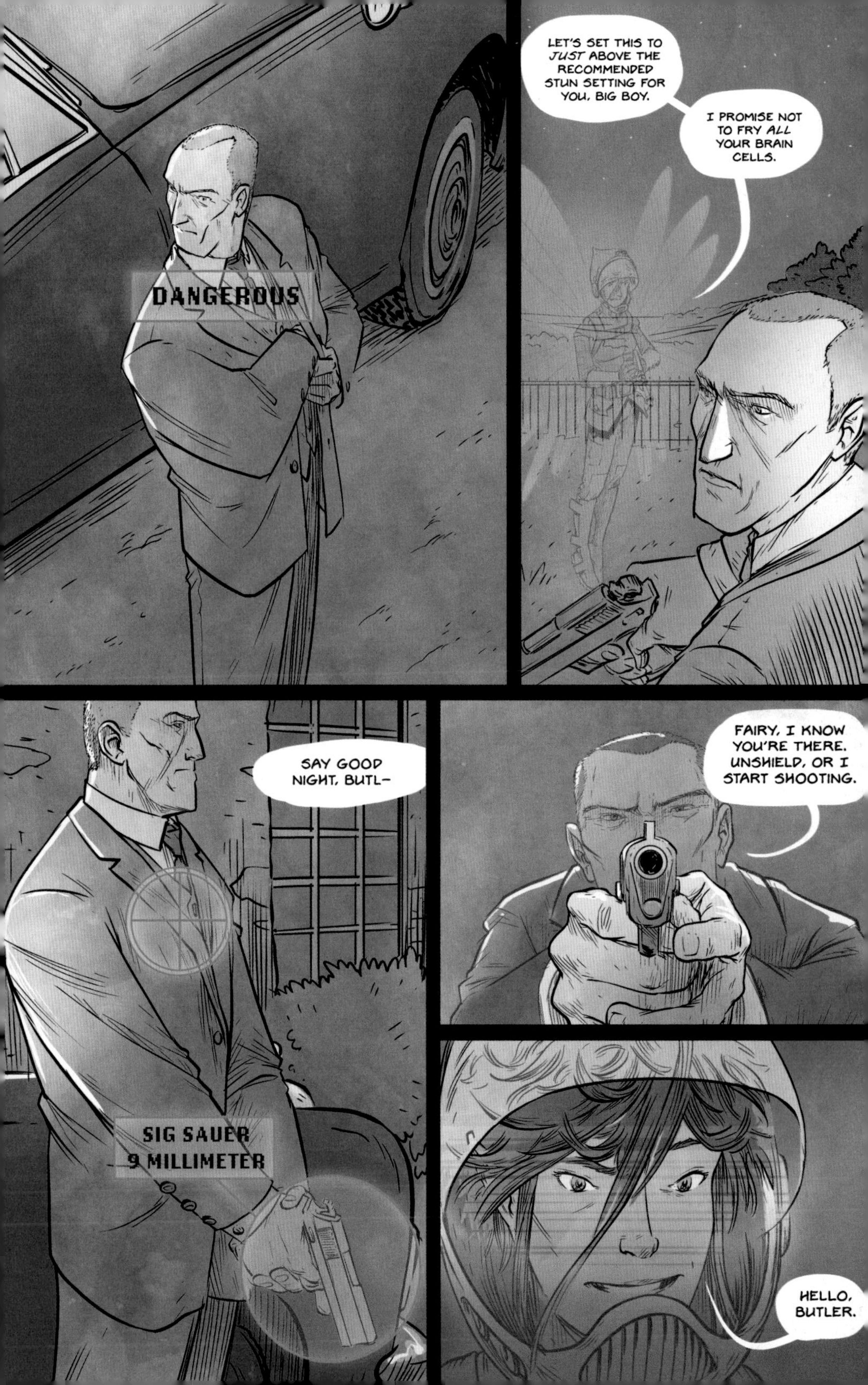
DANGEROUS
LET'S SET THIS TO *JUST* ABOVE THE RECOMMENDED STUN SETTING FOR YOU, BIG BOY.
I PROMISE NOT TO FRY *ALL* YOUR BRAIN CELLS.
SAY GOOD NIGHT, BUTL–
SIG SAUER 9 MILLIMETER
FAIRY, I KNOW YOU'RE THERE. UNSHIELD, OR I START SHOOTING.
HELLO, BUTLER.

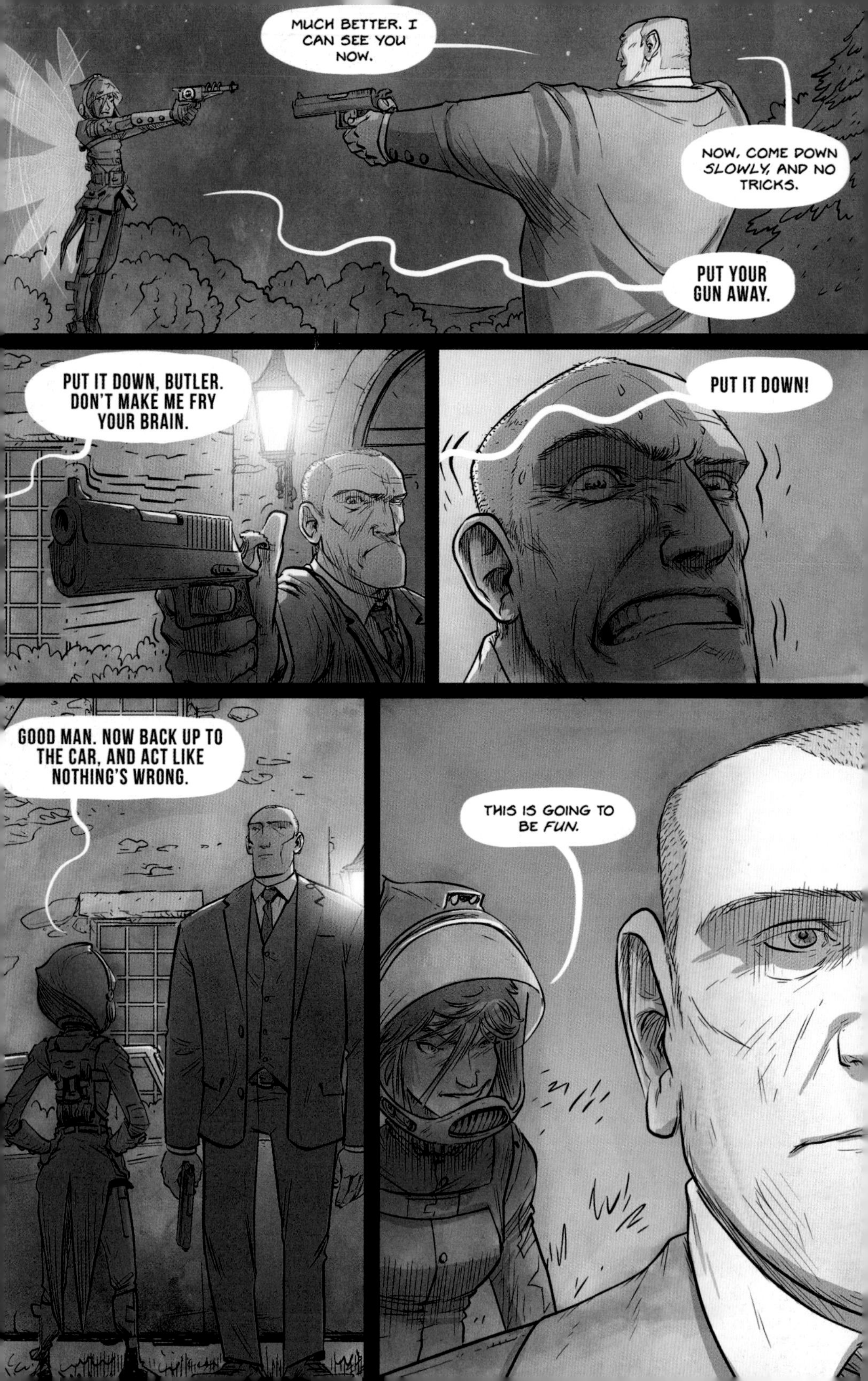

MUCH BETTER. I CAN SEE YOU NOW.
NOW, COME DOWN SLOWLY, AND NO TRICKS.
PUT YOUR GUN AWAY.
PUT IT DOWN, BUTLER. DON'T MAKE ME FRY YOUR BRAIN.
PUT IT DOWN!
GOOD MAN. NOW BACK UP TO THE CAR, AND ACT LIKE NOTHING'S WRONG.
THIS IS GOING TO BE FUN.

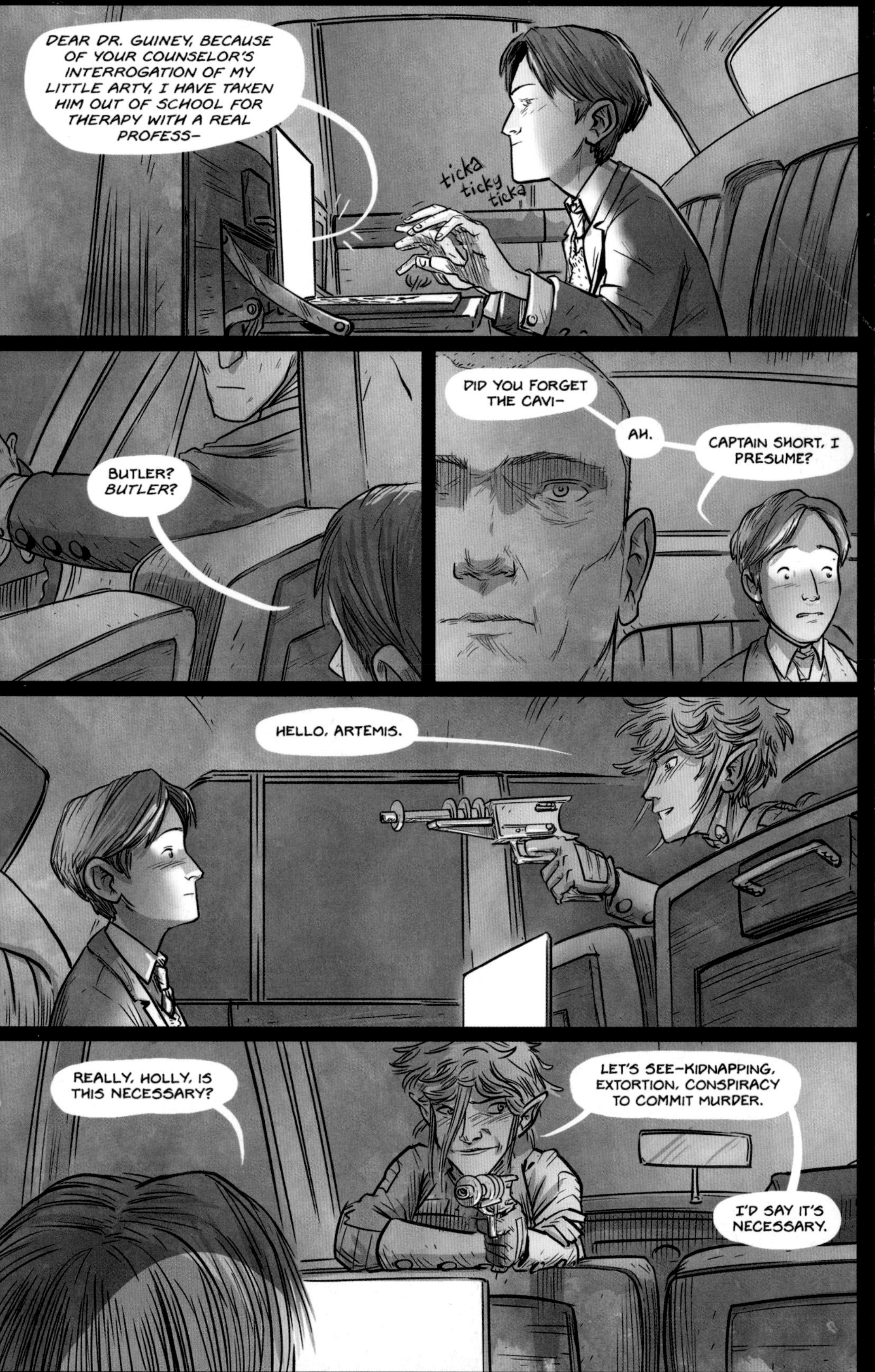
DEAR DR. GUINEY, BECAUSE OF YOUR COUNSELOR'S INTERROGATION OF MY LITTLE ARTY, I HAVE TAKEN HIM OUT OF SCHOOL FOR THERAPY WITH A REAL PROFESS–
ticka ticky ticka
BUTLER? BUTLER?
DID YOU FORGET THE CAVI–
AH.
CAPTAIN SHORT, I PRESUME?
HELLO, ARTEMIS.
REALLY, HOLLY, IS THIS NECESSARY?
LET'S SEE–KIDNAPPING, EXTORTION, CONSPIRACY TO COMMIT MURDER.
I'D SAY IT'S NECESSARY.

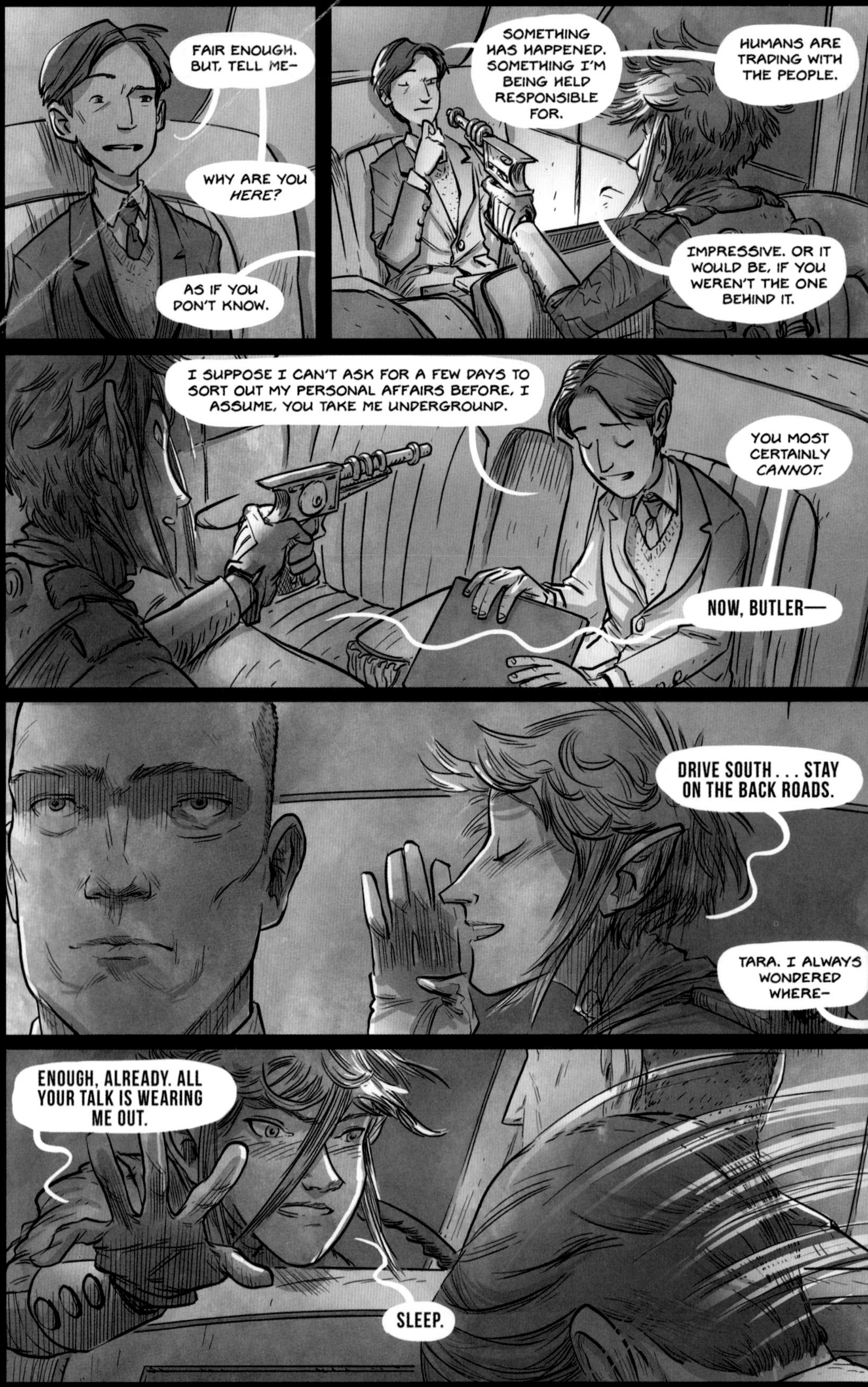
FAIR ENOUGH. BUT, TELL ME-
WHY ARE YOU HERE?
AS IF YOU DON'T KNOW.
SOMETHING HAS HAPPENED. SOMETHING I'M BEING HELD RESPONSIBLE FOR.
HUMANS ARE TRADING WITH THE PEOPLE.
IMPRESSIVE. OR IT WOULD BE, IF YOU WEREN'T THE ONE BEHIND IT.
I SUPPOSE I CAN'T ASK FOR A FEW DAYS TO SORT OUT MY PERSONAL AFFAIRS BEFORE, I ASSUME, YOU TAKE ME UNDERGROUND.
YOU MOST CERTAINLY CANNOT.
NOW, BUTLER—
DRIVE SOUTH . . . STAY ON THE BACK ROADS.
TARA. I ALWAYS WONDERED WHERE-
ENOUGH, ALREADY. ALL YOUR TALK IS WEARING ME OUT.
SLEEP.

CHAPTER FOUR

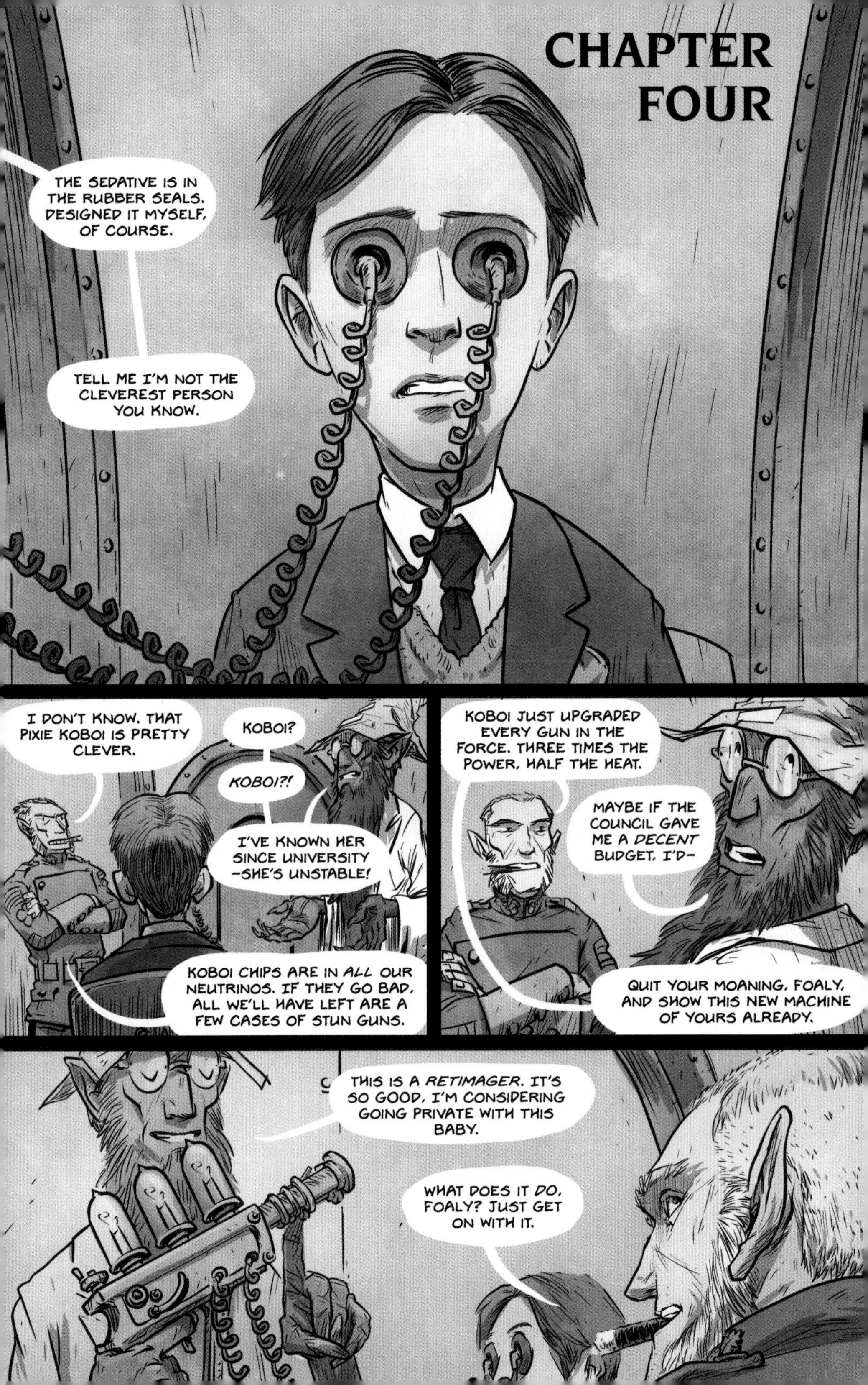
THE SEDATIVE IS IN THE RUBBER SEALS. DESIGNED IT MYSELF, OF COURSE.
TELL ME I'M NOT THE CLEVEREST PERSON YOU KNOW.
I DON'T KNOW. THAT PIXIE KOBOI IS PRETTY CLEVER.
KOBOI?
KOBOI?!
I'VE KNOWN HER SINCE UNIVERSITY —SHE'S UNSTABLE!
KOBOI CHIPS ARE IN ALL OUR NEUTRINOS. IF THEY GO BAD, ALL WE'LL HAVE LEFT ARE A FEW CASES OF STUN GUNS.
KOBOI JUST UPGRADED EVERY GUN IN THE FORCE. THREE TIMES THE POWER, HALF THE HEAT.
MAYBE IF THE COUNCIL GAVE ME A DECENT BUDGET, I'D—
QUIT YOUR MOANING, FOALY, AND SHOW THIS NEW MACHINE OF YOURS ALREADY.
THIS IS A RETIMAGER. IT'S SO GOOD, I'M CONSIDERING GOING PRIVATE WITH THIS BABY.
WHAT DOES IT DO, FOALY? JUST GET ON WITH IT.

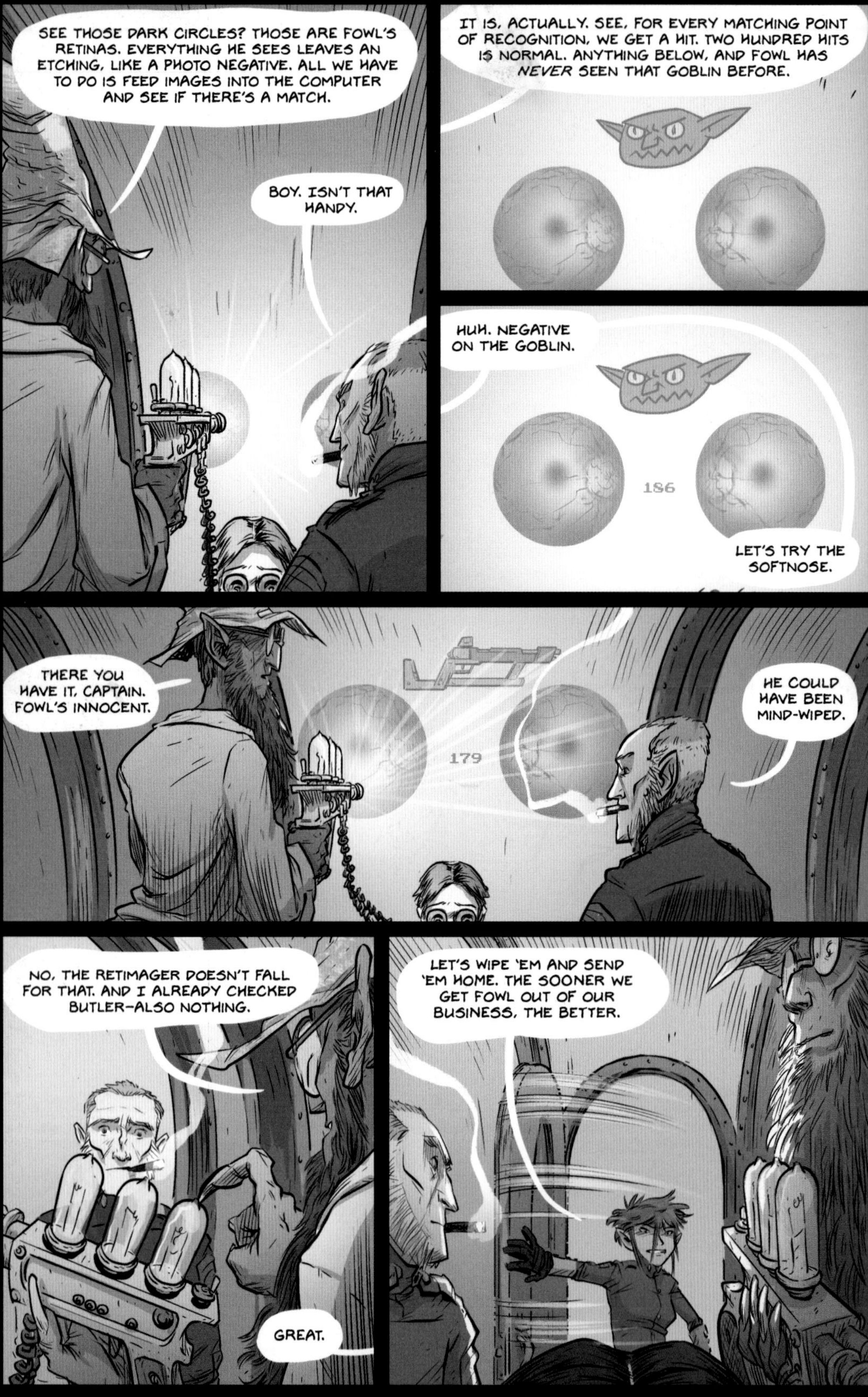
SEE THOSE DARK CIRCLES? THOSE ARE FOWL'S RETINAS. EVERYTHING HE SEES LEAVES AN ETCHING, LIKE A PHOTO NEGATIVE. ALL WE HAVE TO DO IS FEED IMAGES INTO THE COMPUTER AND SEE IF THERE'S A MATCH.
BOY. ISN'T THAT HANDY.
IT IS, ACTUALLY. SEE, FOR EVERY MATCHING POINT OF RECOGNITION, WE GET A HIT. TWO HUNDRED HITS IS NORMAL. ANYTHING BELOW, AND FOWL HAS *NEVER* SEEN THAT GOBLIN BEFORE.
HUH. NEGATIVE ON THE GOBLIN.
186
LET'S TRY THE SOFTNOSE.
THERE YOU HAVE IT, CAPTAIN. FOWL'S INNOCENT.
179
HE COULD HAVE BEEN MIND-WIPED.
NO, THE RETIMAGER DOESN'T FALL FOR THAT. AND I ALREADY CHECKED BUTLER–ALSO NOTHING.
GREAT.
LET'S WIPE 'EM AND SEND 'EM HOME. THE SOONER WE GET FOWL OUT OF OUR BUSINESS, THE BETTER.

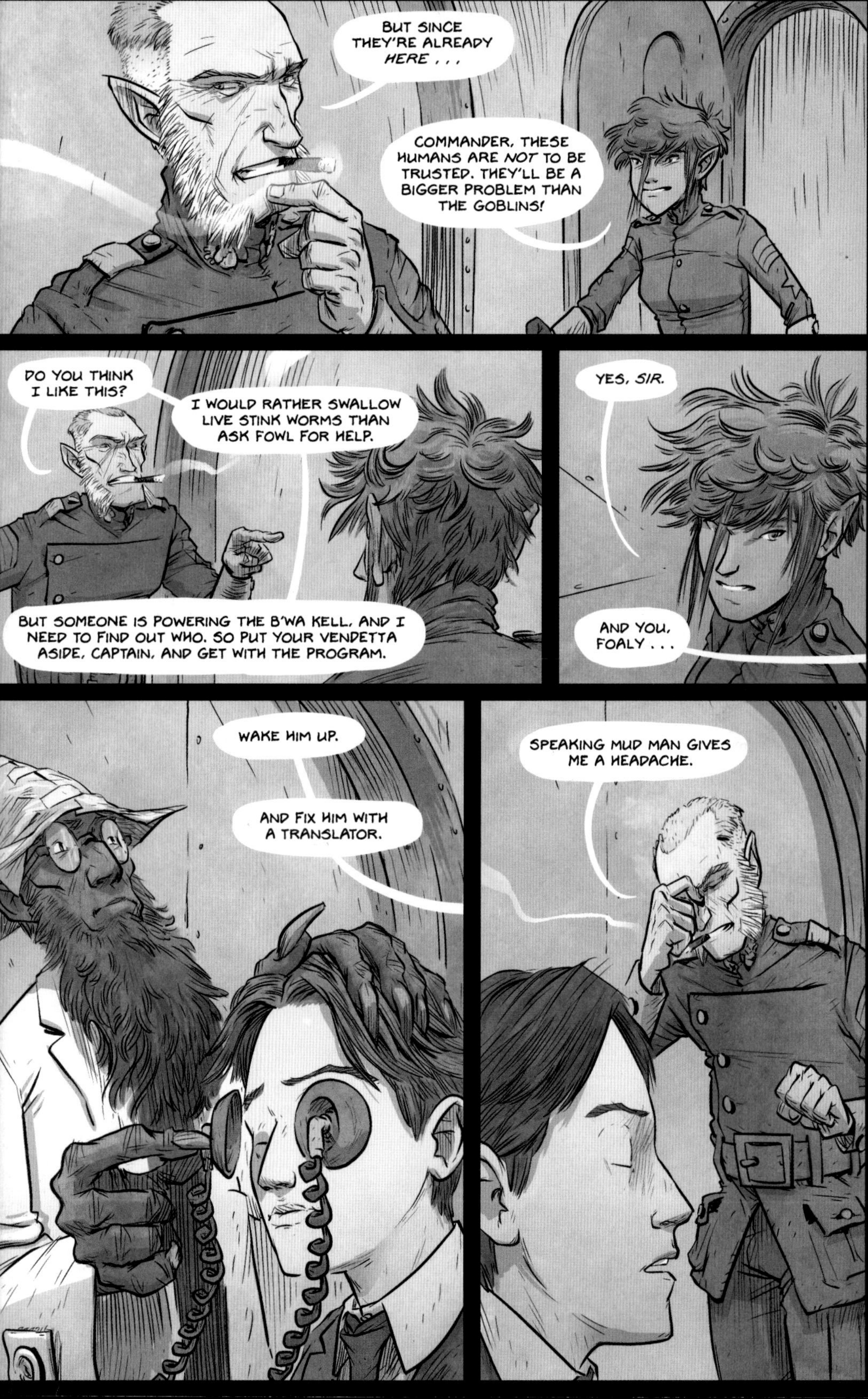
BUT SINCE THEY'RE ALREADY *HERE* . . .
COMMANDER, THESE HUMANS ARE *NOT* TO BE TRUSTED. THEY'LL BE A BIGGER PROBLEM THAN THE GOBLINS!
DO YOU THINK I LIKE THIS?
I WOULD RATHER SWALLOW LIVE STINK WORMS THAN ASK FOWL FOR HELP.
BUT SOMEONE IS POWERING THE B'WA KELL, AND I NEED TO FIND OUT WHO. SO PUT YOUR VENDETTA ASIDE, CAPTAIN, AND GET WITH THE PROGRAM.
YES, *SIR*.
AND YOU, FOALY . . .
WAKE HIM UP.
AND FIX HIM WITH A TRANSLATOR.
SPEAKING MUD MAN GIVES ME A HEADACHE.

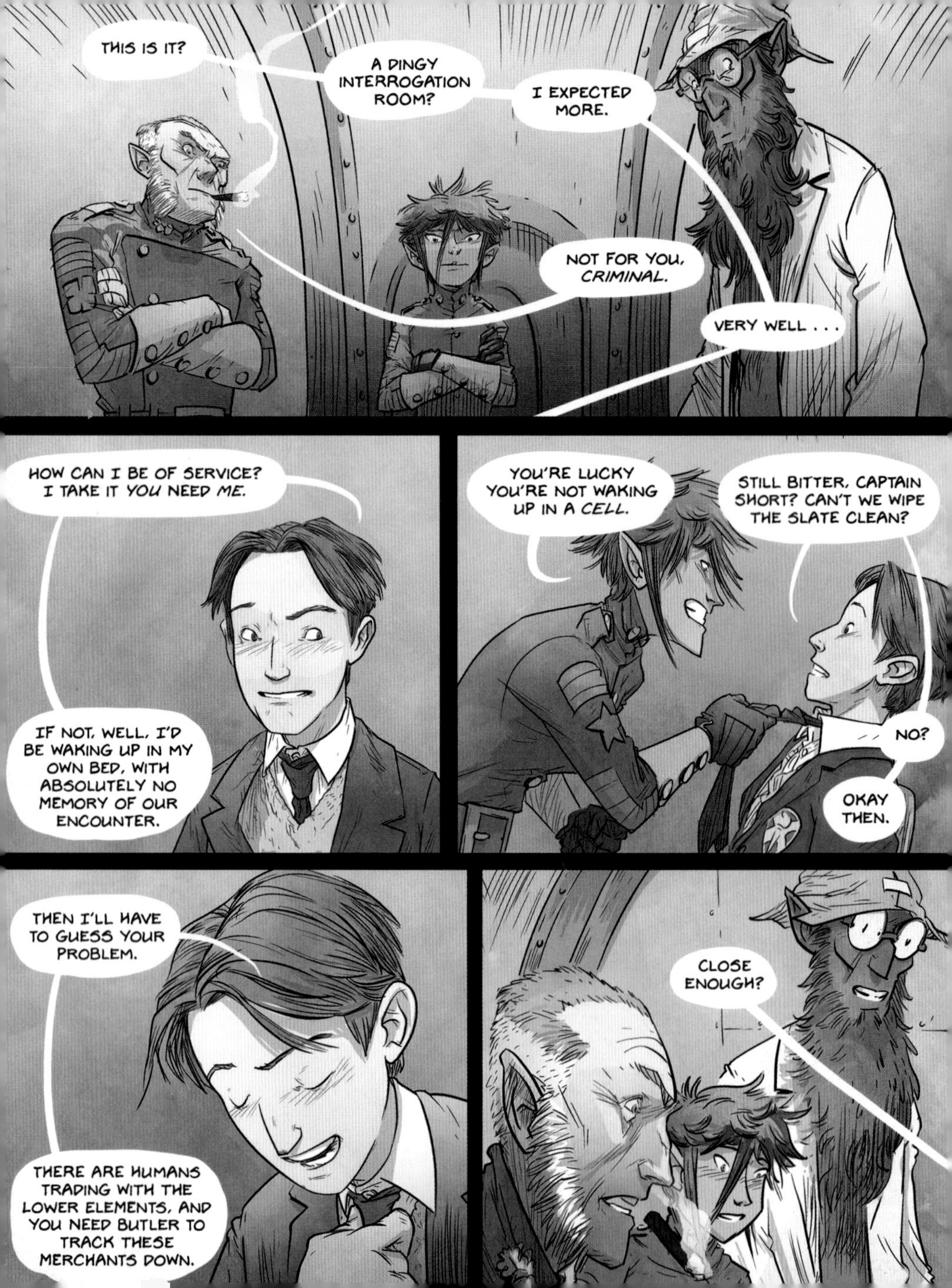

THIS IS IT?
A DINGY INTERROGATION ROOM?
I EXPECTED MORE.
NOT FOR YOU, *CRIMINAL.*
VERY WELL . . .
HOW CAN I BE OF SERVICE? I TAKE IT *YOU* NEED *ME.*
IF NOT, WELL, I'D BE WAKING UP IN MY OWN BED, WITH ABSOLUTELY NO MEMORY OF OUR ENCOUNTER.
YOU'RE LUCKY YOU'RE NOT WAKING UP IN A *CELL.*
STILL BITTER, CAPTAIN SHORT? CAN'T WE WIPE THE SLATE CLEAN?
NO?
OKAY THEN.
THEN I'LL HAVE TO GUESS YOUR PROBLEM.
THERE ARE HUMANS TRADING WITH THE LOWER ELEMENTS, AND YOU NEED BUTLER TO TRACK THESE MERCHANTS DOWN.
CLOSE ENOUGH?

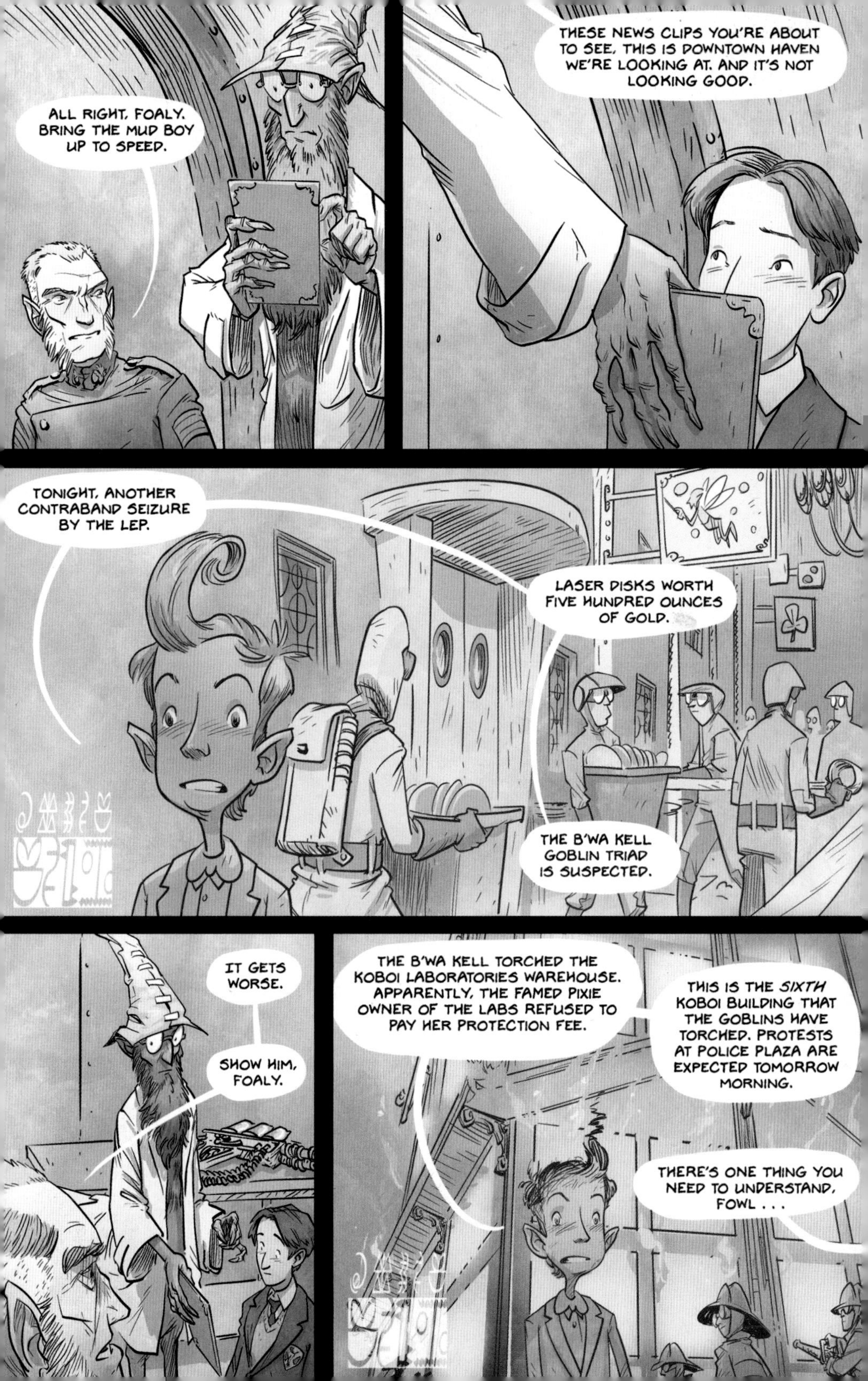
ALL RIGHT, FOALY. BRING THE MUD BOY UP TO SPEED.
THESE NEWS CLIPS YOU'RE ABOUT TO SEE, THIS IS DOWNTOWN HAVEN WE'RE LOOKING AT. AND IT'S NOT LOOKING GOOD.
TONIGHT, ANOTHER CONTRABAND SEIZURE BY THE LEP.
LASER DISKS WORTH FIVE HUNDRED OUNCES OF GOLD.
THE B'WA KELL GOBLIN TRIAD IS SUSPECTED.
IT GETS WORSE.
SHOW HIM, FOALY.
THE B'WA KELL TORCHED THE KOBOI LABORATORIES WAREHOUSE. APPARENTLY, THE FAMED PIXIE OWNER OF THE LABS REFUSED TO PAY HER PROTECTION FEE.
THIS IS THE *SIXTH* KOBOI BUILDING THAT THE GOBLINS HAVE TORCHED. PROTESTS AT POLICE PLAZA ARE EXPECTED TOMORROW MORNING.
THERE'S ONE THING YOU NEED TO UNDERSTAND, FOWL . . .

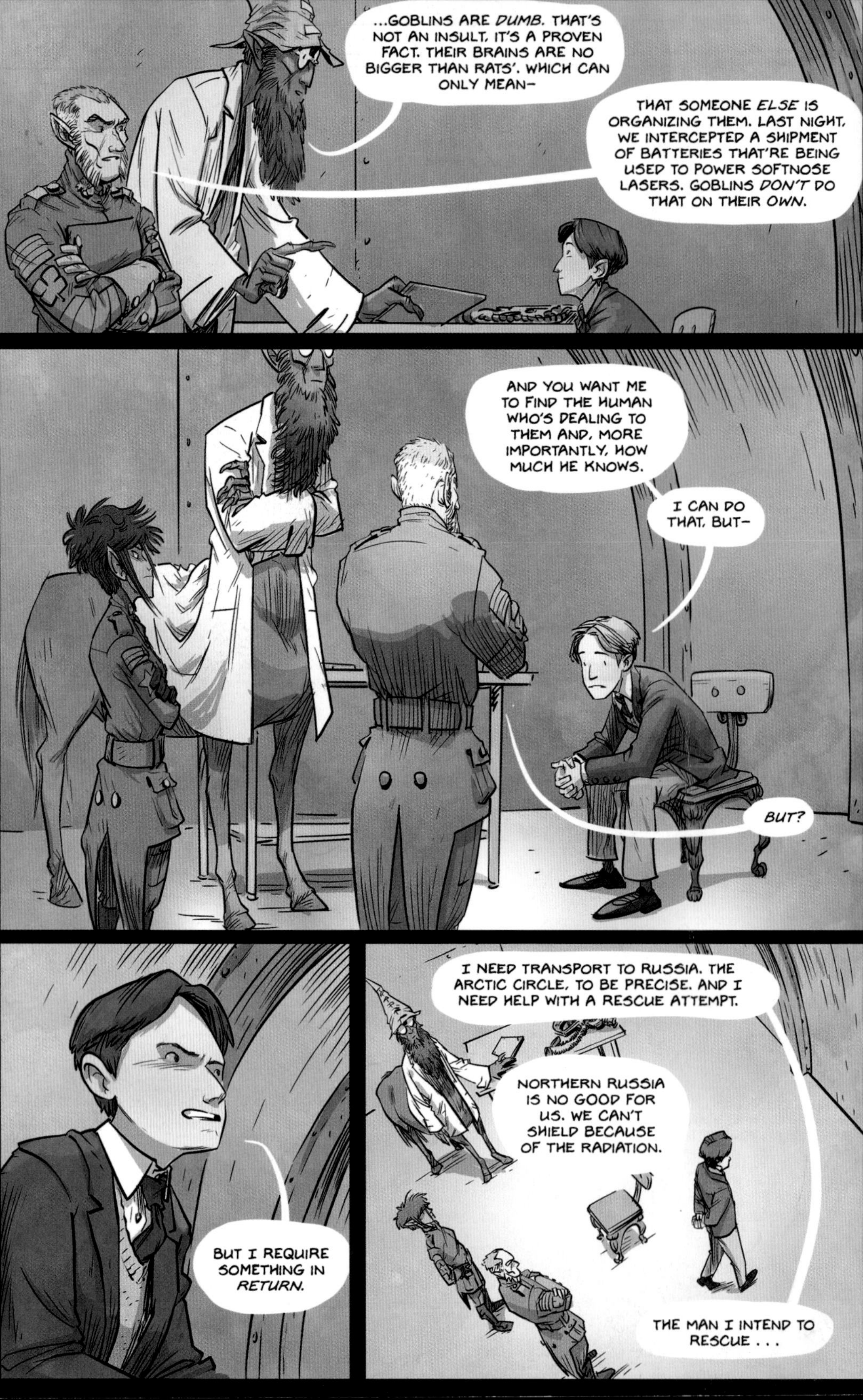
...GOBLINS ARE *DUMB*. THAT'S NOT AN INSULT, IT'S A PROVEN FACT. THEIR BRAINS ARE NO BIGGER THAN RATS'. WHICH CAN ONLY MEAN–
THAT SOMEONE *ELSE* IS ORGANIZING THEM. LAST NIGHT, WE INTERCEPTED A SHIPMENT OF BATTERIES THAT'RE BEING USED TO POWER SOFTNOSE LASERS. GOBLINS *DON'T* DO THAT ON THEIR *OWN*.
AND YOU WANT ME TO FIND THE HUMAN WHO'S DEALING TO THEM AND, MORE IMPORTANTLY, HOW MUCH HE KNOWS.
I CAN DO THAT, BUT–
BUT?
BUT I REQUIRE SOMETHING IN *RETURN*.
I NEED TRANSPORT TO RUSSIA. THE ARCTIC CIRCLE, TO BE PRECISE. AND I NEED HELP WITH A RESCUE ATTEMPT.
NORTHERN RUSSIA IS NO GOOD FOR US. WE CAN'T SHIELD BECAUSE OF THE RADIATION.
THE MAN I INTEND TO RESCUE . . .

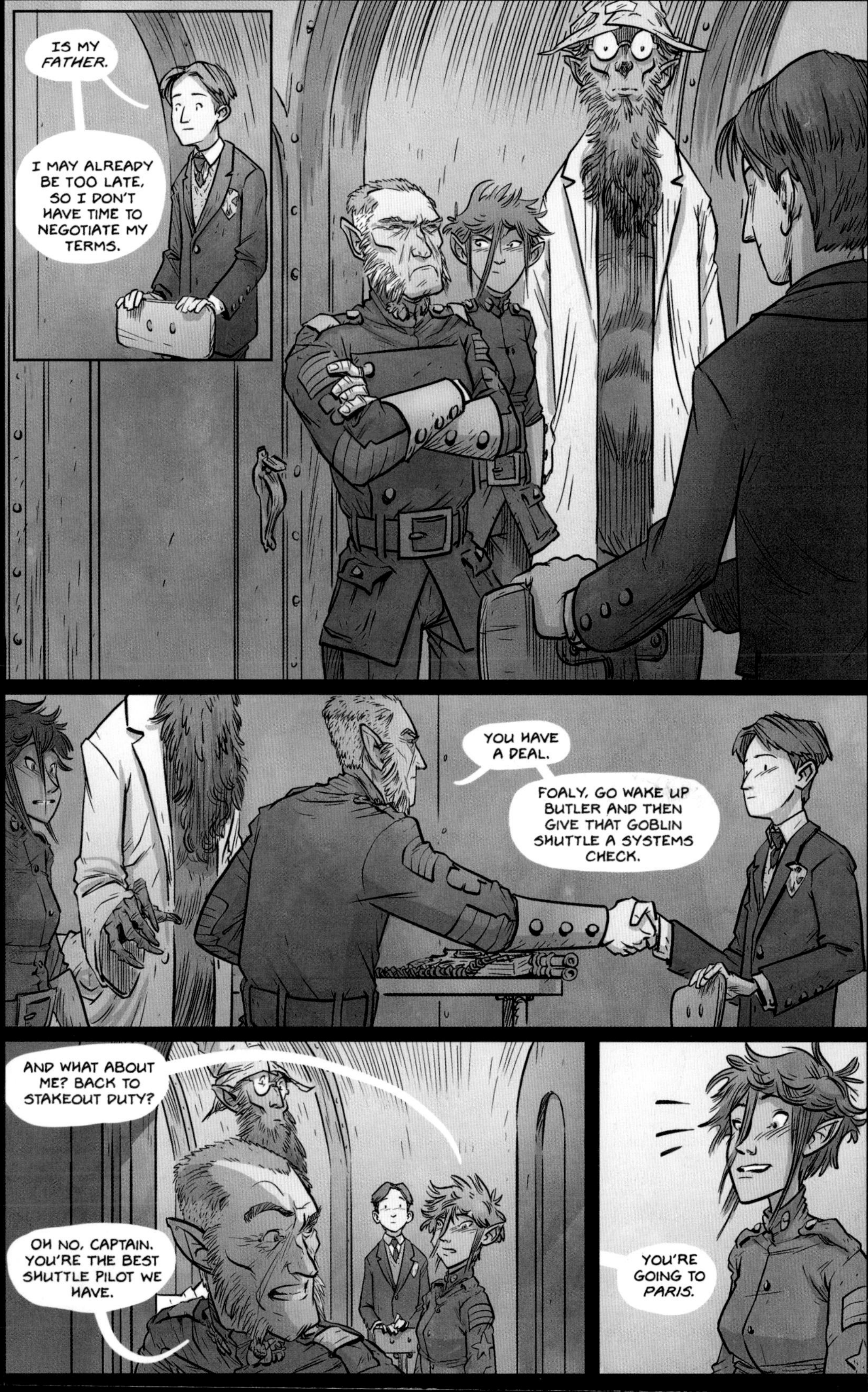
IS MY *FATHER.*
I MAY ALREADY BE TOO LATE, SO I DON'T HAVE TIME TO NEGOTIATE MY TERMS.
YOU HAVE A DEAL.
FOALY, GO WAKE UP BUTLER AND THEN GIVE THAT GOBLIN SHUTTLE A SYSTEMS CHECK.
AND WHAT ABOUT ME? BACK TO STAKEOUT DUTY?
OH NO, CAPTAIN. YOU'RE THE BEST SHUTTLE PILOT WE HAVE.
YOU'RE GOING TO *PARIS.*

CHAPTER FIVE

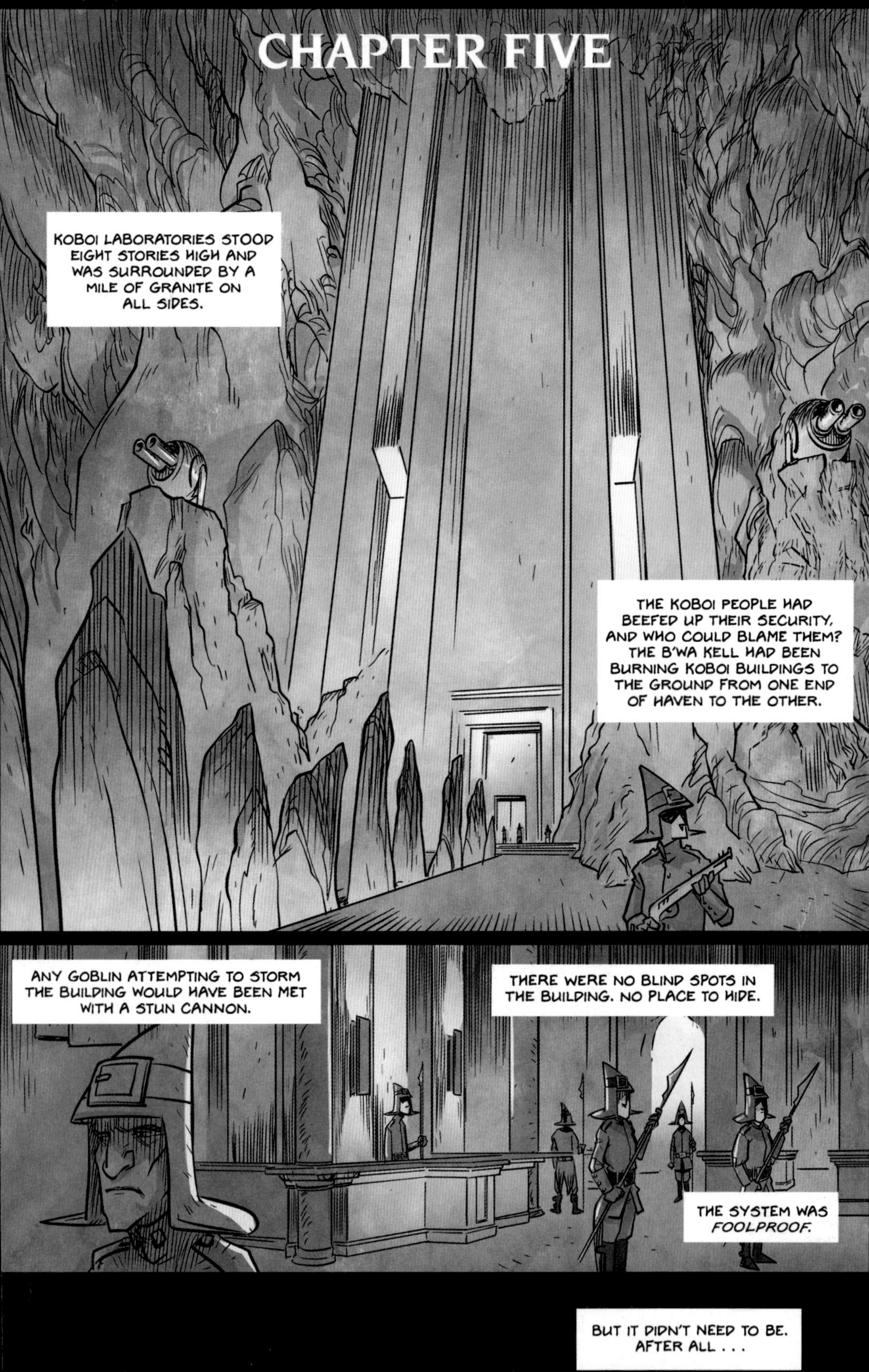
KOBOI LABORATORIES STOOD EIGHT STORIES HIGH AND WAS SURROUNDED BY A MILE OF GRANITE ON ALL SIDES.
THE KOBOI PEOPLE HAD BEEFED UP THEIR SECURITY, AND WHO COULD BLAME THEM? THE B'WA KELL HAD BEEN BURNING KOBOI BUILDINGS TO THE GROUND FROM ONE END OF HAVEN TO THE OTHER.
ANY GOBLIN ATTEMPTING TO STORM THE BUILDING WOULD HAVE BEEN MET WITH A STUN CANNON.
THERE WERE NO BLIND SPOTS IN THE BUILDING. NO PLACE TO HIDE.
THE SYSTEM WAS *FOOLPROOF.*
BUT IT DIDN'T NEED TO BE. AFTER ALL . . .

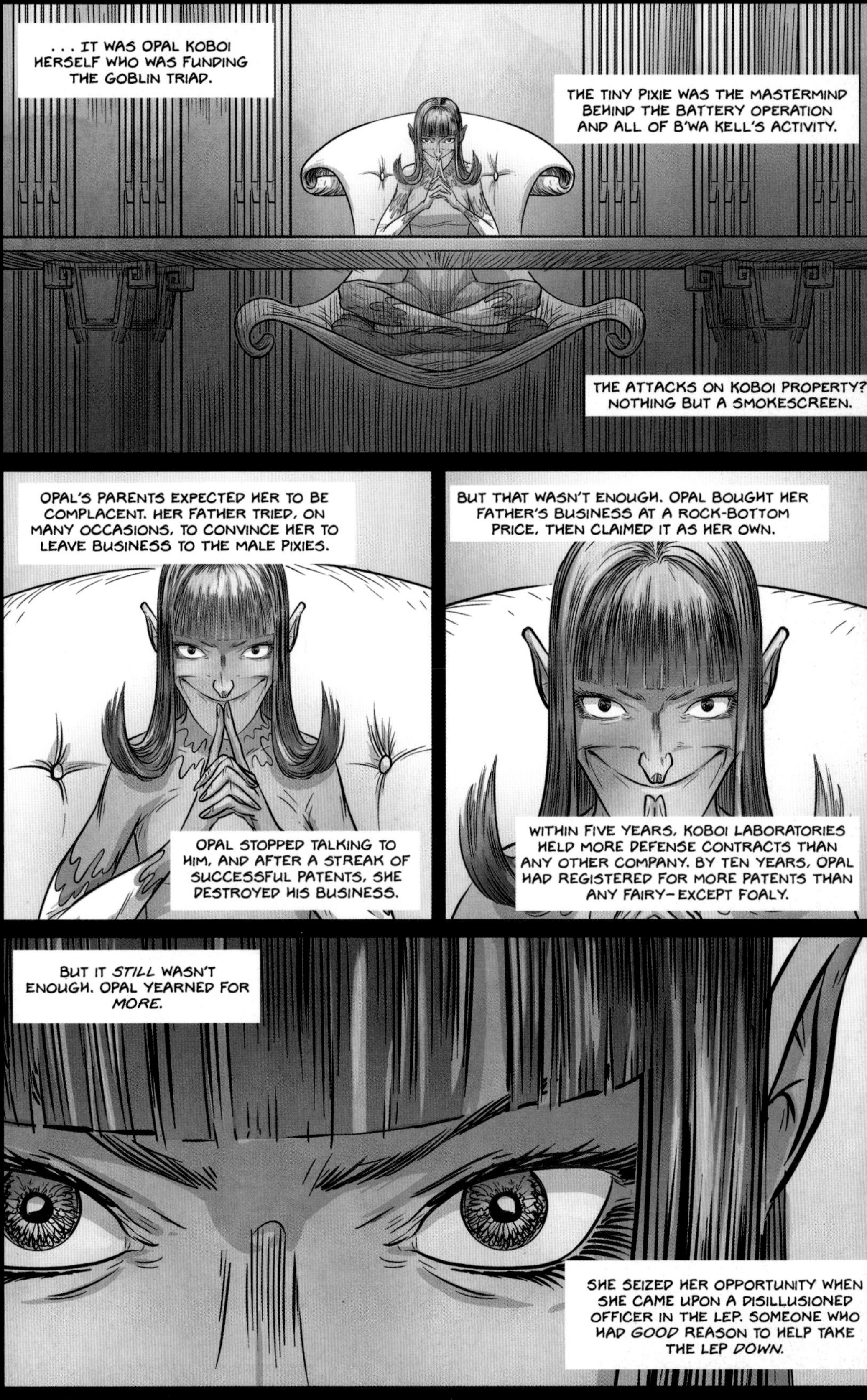
. . . IT WAS OPAL KOBOI HERSELF WHO WAS FUNDING THE GOBLIN TRIAD.
THE TINY PIXIE WAS THE MASTERMIND BEHIND THE BATTERY OPERATION AND ALL OF B'WA KELL'S ACTIVITY.
THE ATTACKS ON KOBOI PROPERTY? NOTHING BUT A SMOKESCREEN.
OPAL'S PARENTS EXPECTED HER TO BE COMPLACENT. HER FATHER TRIED, ON MANY OCCASIONS, TO CONVINCE HER TO LEAVE BUSINESS TO THE MALE PIXIES.
OPAL STOPPED TALKING TO HIM, AND AFTER A STREAK OF SUCCESSFUL PATENTS, SHE DESTROYED HIS BUSINESS.
BUT THAT WASN'T ENOUGH. OPAL BOUGHT HER FATHER'S BUSINESS AT A ROCK-BOTTOM PRICE, THEN CLAIMED IT AS HER OWN.
WITHIN FIVE YEARS, KOBOI LABORATORIES HELD MORE DEFENSE CONTRACTS THAN ANY OTHER COMPANY. BY TEN YEARS, OPAL HAD REGISTERED FOR MORE PATENTS THAN ANY FAIRY—EXCEPT FOALY.
BUT IT *STILL* WASN'T ENOUGH. OPAL YEARNED FOR *MORE.*
SHE SEIZED HER OPPORTUNITY WHEN SHE CAME UPON A DISILLUSIONED OFFICER IN THE LEP. SOMEONE WHO HAD *GOOD* REASON TO HELP TAKE THE LEP *DOWN.*

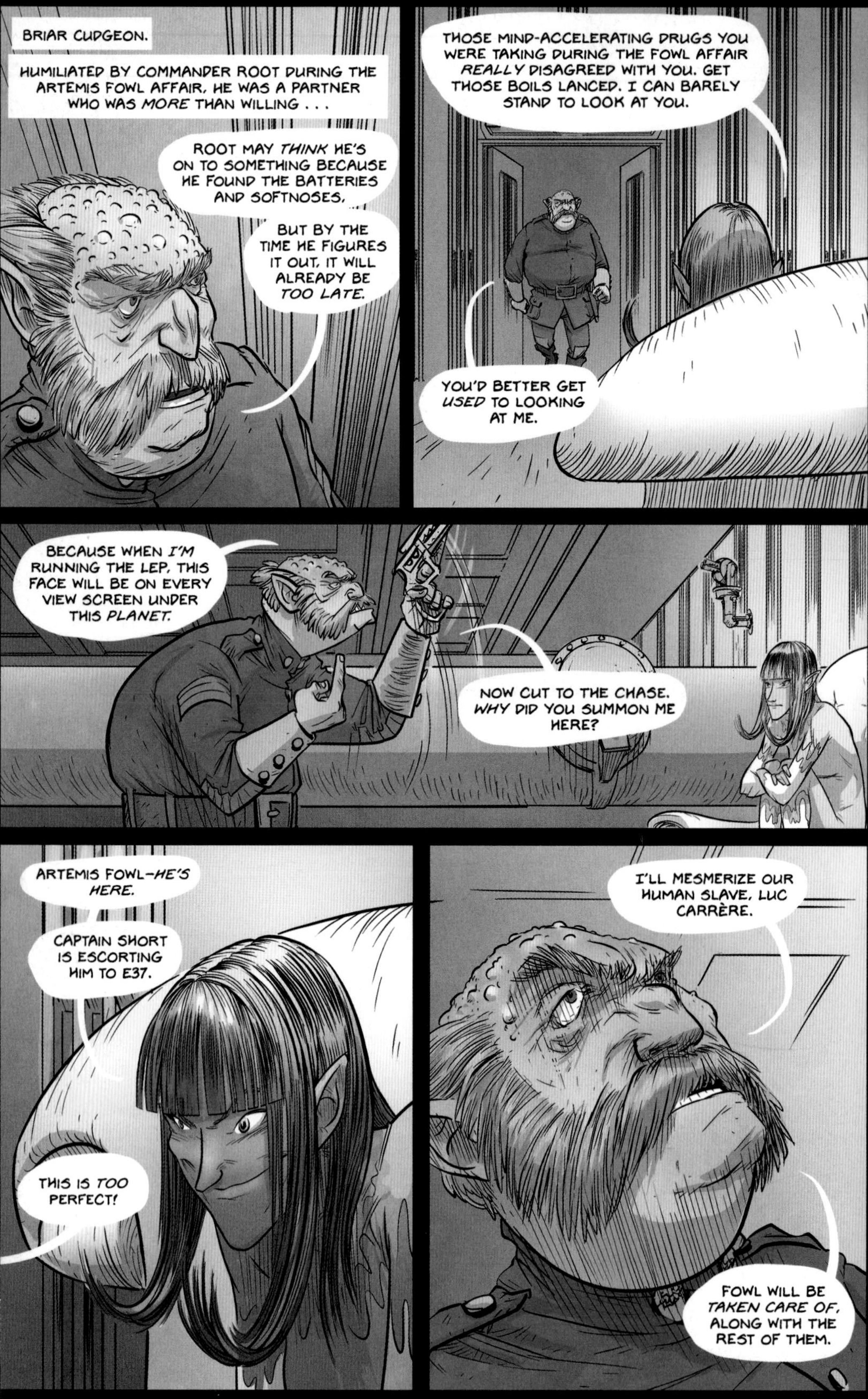
BRIAR CUDGEON.
HUMILIATED BY COMMANDER ROOT DURING THE ARTEMIS FOWL AFFAIR, HE WAS A PARTNER WHO WAS *MORE* THAN WILLING . . .
ROOT MAY *THINK* HE'S ON TO SOMETHING BECAUSE HE FOUND THE BATTERIES AND SOFTNOSES,
BUT BY THE TIME HE FIGURES IT OUT, IT WILL ALREADY BE *TOO LATE.*
THOSE MIND-ACCELERATING DRUGS YOU WERE TAKING DURING THE FOWL AFFAIR *REALLY* DISAGREED WITH YOU. GET THOSE BOILS LANCED. I CAN BARELY STAND TO LOOK AT YOU.
YOU'D BETTER GET *USED* TO LOOKING AT ME.
BECAUSE WHEN *I'M* RUNNING THE LEP, THIS FACE WILL BE ON EVERY VIEW SCREEN UNDER THIS *PLANET.*
NOW CUT TO THE CHASE. *WHY* DID YOU SUMMON ME HERE?
ARTEMIS FOWL—*HE'S HERE.*
CAPTAIN SHORT IS ESCORTING HIM TO E37.
THIS IS *TOO* PERFECT!
I'LL MESMERIZE OUR HUMAN SLAVE, LUC CARRÈRE.
FOWL WILL BE *TAKEN CARE OF,* ALONG WITH THE REST OF THEM.

CHAPTER SIX

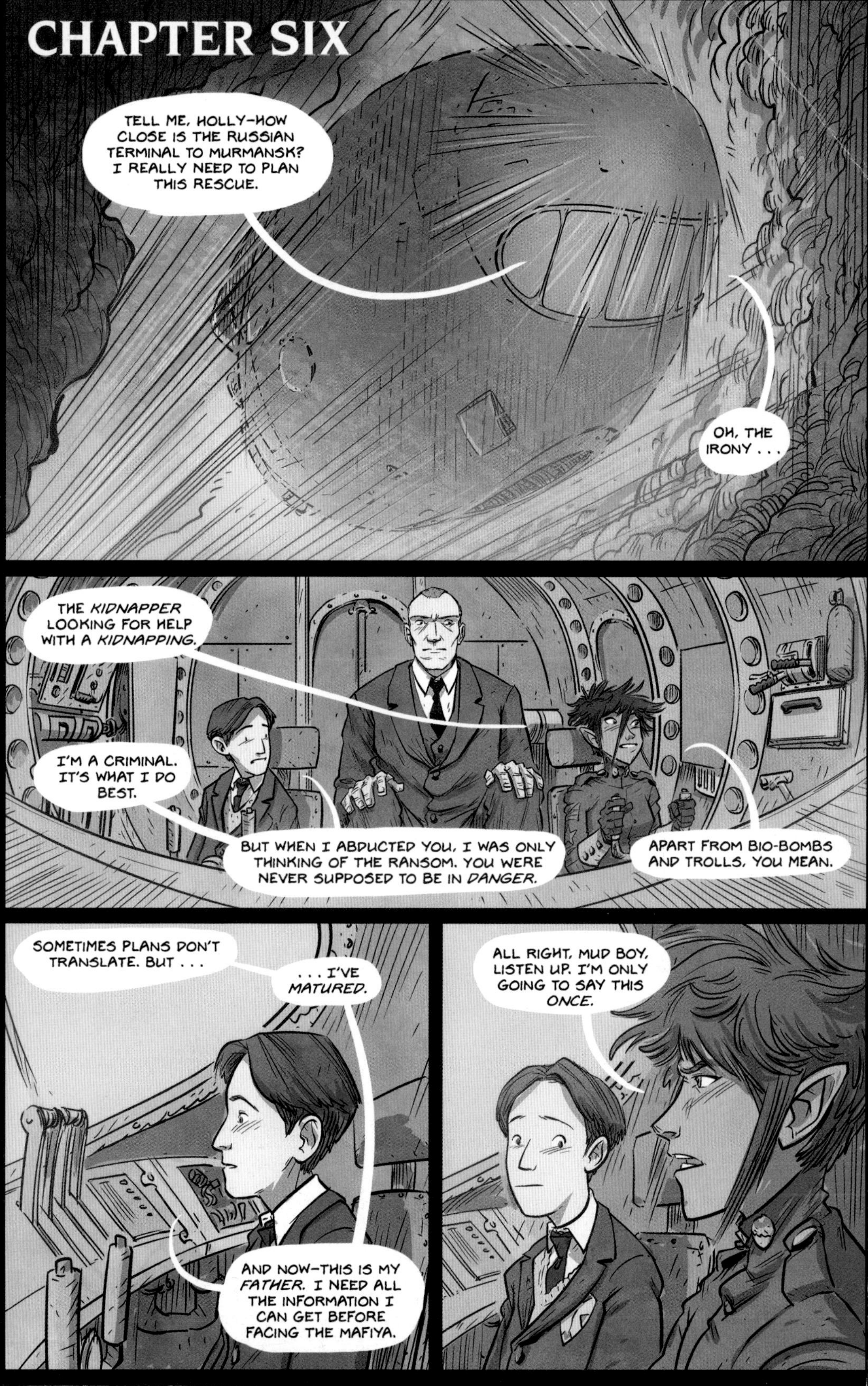

TELL ME, HOLLY—HOW CLOSE IS THE RUSSIAN TERMINAL TO MURMANSK? I REALLY NEED TO PLAN THIS RESCUE.
OH, THE IRONY . . .
THE *KIDNAPPER* LOOKING FOR HELP WITH A *KIDNAPPING*.
I'M A CRIMINAL. IT'S WHAT I DO BEST.
BUT WHEN I ABDUCTED YOU, I WAS ONLY THINKING OF THE RANSOM. YOU WERE NEVER SUPPOSED TO BE IN *DANGER*.
APART FROM BIO-BOMBS AND TROLLS, YOU MEAN.
SOMETIMES PLANS DON'T TRANSLATE. BUT . . .
. . . I'VE *MATURED*.
AND NOW—THIS IS MY *FATHER*. I NEED ALL THE INFORMATION I CAN GET BEFORE FACING THE MAFIYA.
ALL RIGHT, MUD BOY, LISTEN UP. I'M ONLY GOING TO SAY THIS *ONCE*.

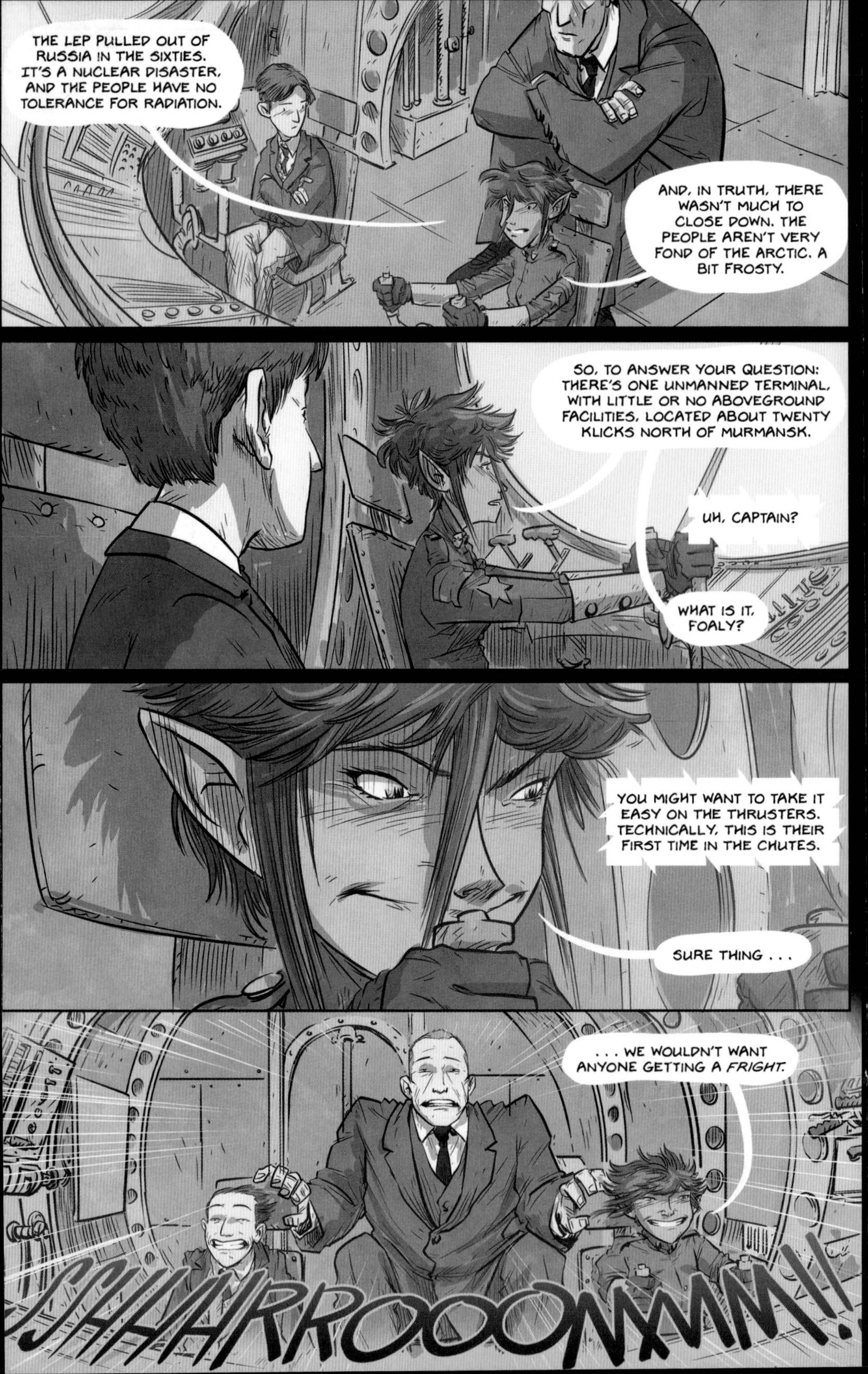
THE LEP PULLED OUT OF RUSSIA IN THE SIXTIES. IT'S A NUCLEAR DISASTER, AND THE PEOPLE HAVE NO TOLERANCE FOR RADIATION.
AND, IN TRUTH, THERE WASN'T MUCH TO CLOSE DOWN. THE PEOPLE AREN'T VERY FOND OF THE ARCTIC. A BIT FROSTY.
SO, TO ANSWER YOUR QUESTION: THERE'S ONE UNMANNED TERMINAL, WITH LITTLE OR NO ABOVEGROUND FACILITIES, LOCATED ABOUT TWENTY KLICKS NORTH OF MURMANSK.
UH, CAPTAIN?
WHAT IS IT, FOALY?
YOU MIGHT WANT TO TAKE IT EASY ON THE THRUSTERS. TECHNICALLY, THIS IS THEIR FIRST TIME IN THE CHUTES.
SURE THING . . .
. . . WE WOULDN'T WANT ANYONE GETTING A *FRIGHT.*
SHHRROOOMMM!!

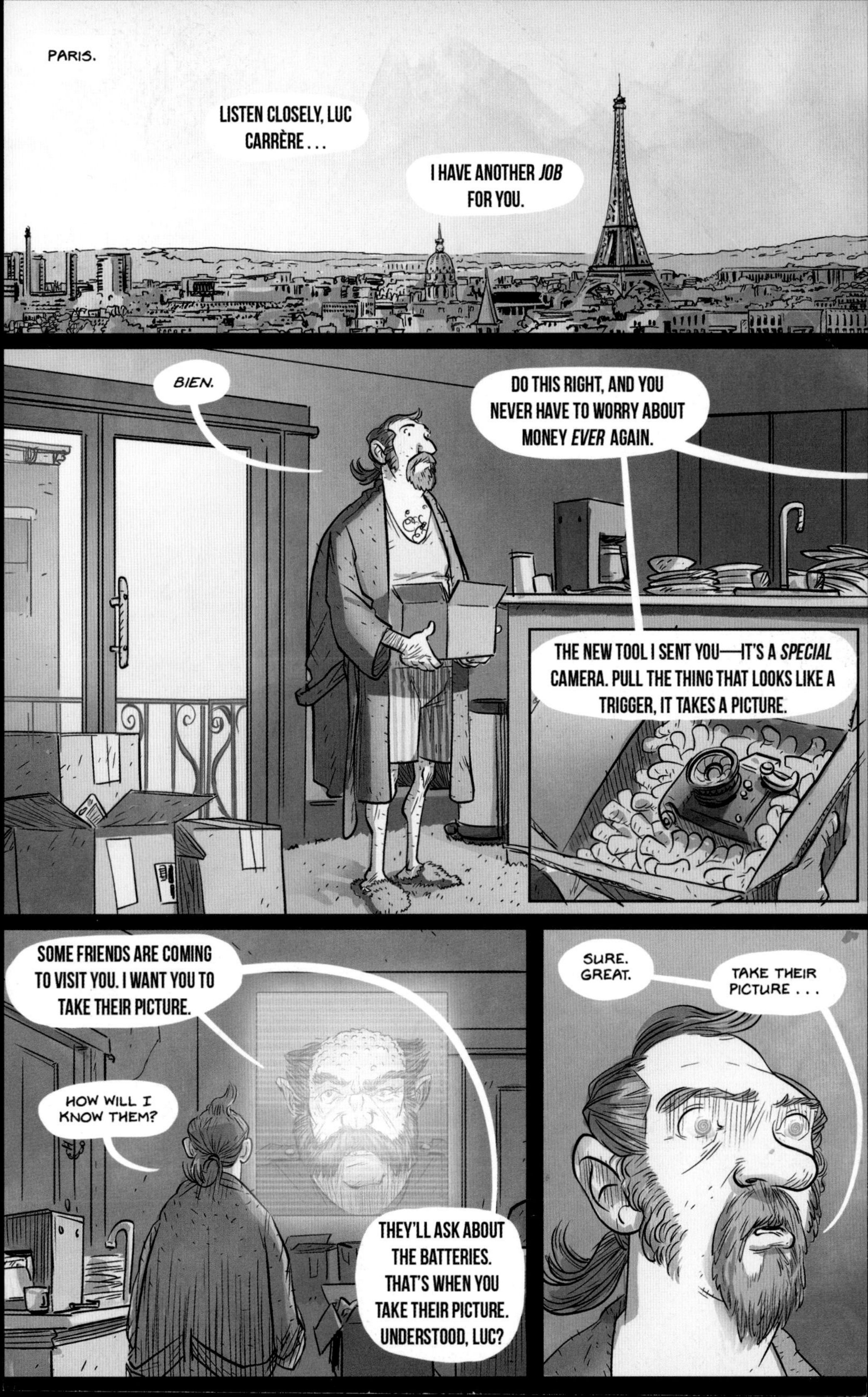

PARIS.
LISTEN CLOSELY, LUC CARRÈRE . . .
I HAVE ANOTHER *JOB* FOR YOU.
BIEN.
DO THIS RIGHT, AND YOU NEVER HAVE TO WORRY ABOUT MONEY *EVER* AGAIN.
THE NEW TOOL I SENT YOU—IT'S A *SPECIAL* CAMERA. PULL THE THING THAT LOOKS LIKE A TRIGGER, IT TAKES A PICTURE.
SOME FRIENDS ARE COMING TO VISIT YOU. I WANT YOU TO TAKE THEIR PICTURE.
HOW WILL I KNOW THEM?
THEY'LL ASK ABOUT THE BATTERIES. THAT'S WHEN YOU TAKE THEIR PICTURE. UNDERSTOOD, LUC?
SURE. GREAT.
TAKE THEIR PICTURE . . .

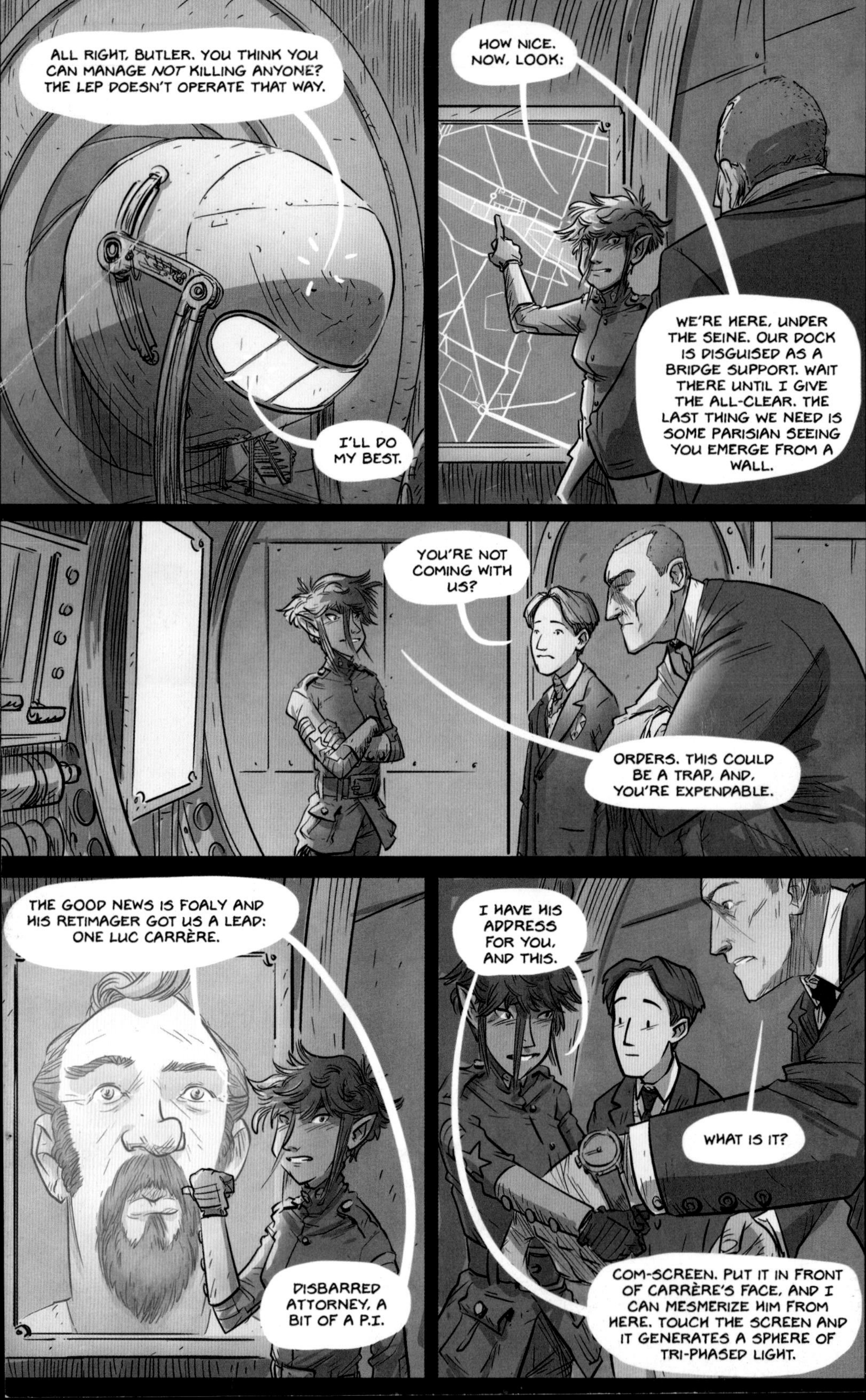

ALL RIGHT, BUTLER. YOU THINK YOU CAN MANAGE *NOT* KILLING ANYONE? THE LEP DOESN'T OPERATE THAT WAY.
I'LL DO MY BEST.
HOW NICE. NOW, LOOK:
WE'RE HERE, UNDER THE SEINE. OUR DOCK IS DISGUISED AS A BRIDGE SUPPORT. WAIT THERE UNTIL I GIVE THE ALL-CLEAR. THE LAST THING WE NEED IS SOME PARISIAN SEEING YOU EMERGE FROM A WALL.
YOU'RE NOT COMING WITH US?
ORDERS. THIS COULD BE A TRAP, AND, YOU'RE EXPENDABLE.
THE GOOD NEWS IS FOALY AND HIS RETIMAGER GOT US A LEAD: ONE LUC CARRÈRE.
DISBARRED ATTORNEY, A BIT OF A P.I.
I HAVE HIS ADDRESS FOR YOU, AND THIS.
WHAT IS IT?
COM-SCREEN. PUT IT IN FRONT OF CARRÈRE'S FACE, AND I CAN MESMERIZE HIM FROM HERE. TOUCH THE SCREEN AND IT GENERATES A SPHERE OF TRI-PHASED LIGHT.

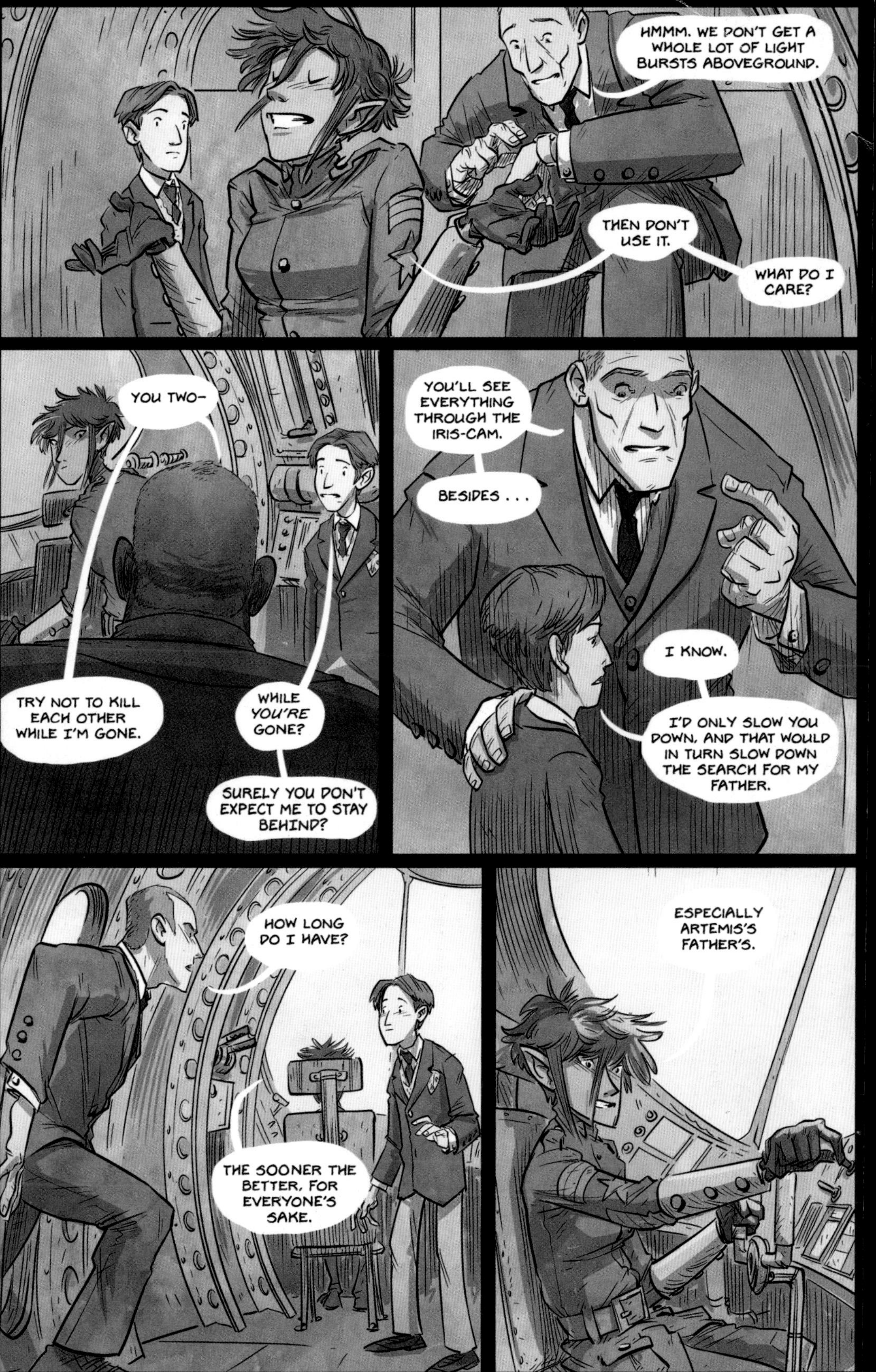
HMMM. WE DON'T GET A WHOLE LOT OF LIGHT BURSTS ABOVEGROUND.
THEN DON'T USE IT.
WHAT DO I CARE?
YOU TWO-
TRY NOT TO KILL EACH OTHER WHILE I'M GONE.
WHILE *YOU'RE* GONE?
SURELY YOU DON'T EXPECT ME TO STAY BEHIND?
YOU'LL SEE EVERYTHING THROUGH THE IRIS-CAM.
BESIDES . . .
I KNOW.
I'D ONLY SLOW YOU DOWN, AND THAT WOULD IN TURN SLOW DOWN THE SEARCH FOR MY FATHER.
HOW LONG DO I HAVE?
THE SOONER THE BETTER, FOR EVERYONE'S SAKE.
ESPECIALLY ARTEMIS'S FATHER'S.

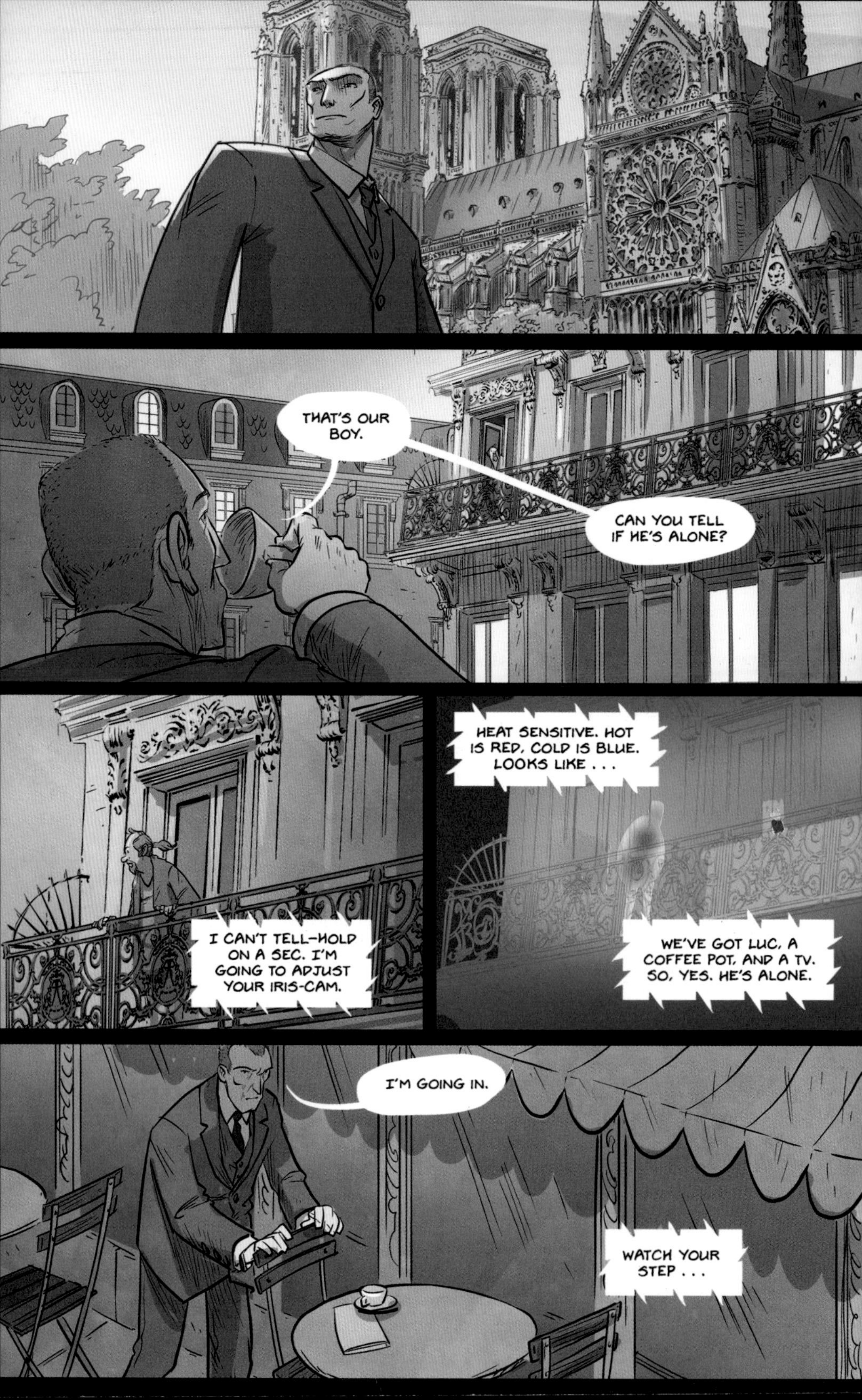
THAT'S OUR BOY.
CAN YOU TELL IF HE'S ALONE?
I CAN'T TELL—HOLD ON A SEC. I'M GOING TO ADJUST YOUR IRIS-CAM.
HEAT SENSITIVE. HOT IS RED, COLD IS BLUE. LOOKS LIKE . . .
WE'VE GOT LUC, A COFFEE POT, AND A TV. SO, YES. HE'S ALONE.
I'M GOING IN.
WATCH YOUR STEP . . .

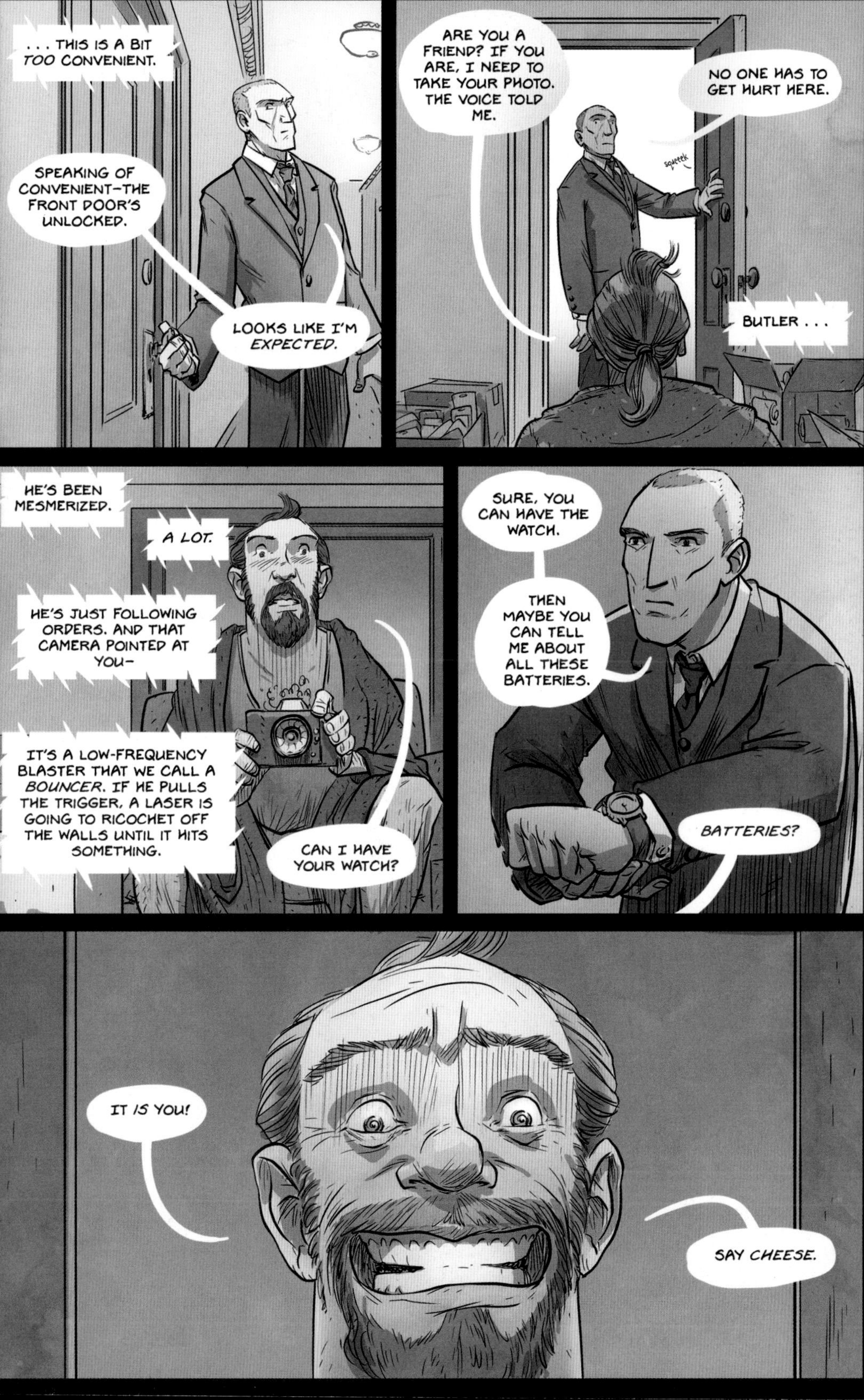

. . . THIS IS A BIT *TOO* CONVENIENT.
SPEAKING OF CONVENIENT—THE FRONT DOOR'S UNLOCKED.
LOOKS LIKE I'M *EXPECTED*.
ARE YOU A FRIEND? IF YOU ARE, I NEED TO TAKE YOUR PHOTO. THE VOICE TOLD ME.
squeeek
NO ONE HAS TO GET HURT HERE.
BUTLER . . .
HE'S BEEN MESMERIZED.
A LOT.
HE'S JUST FOLLOWING ORDERS. AND THAT CAMERA POINTED AT YOU—
IT'S A LOW-FREQUENCY BLASTER THAT WE CALL A *BOUNCER*. IF HE PULLS THE TRIGGER, A LASER IS GOING TO RICOCHET OFF THE WALLS UNTIL IT HITS SOMETHING.
CAN I HAVE YOUR WATCH?
SURE, YOU CAN HAVE THE WATCH.
THEN MAYBE YOU CAN TELL ME ABOUT ALL THESE BATTERIES.
BATTERIES?
IT *IS* YOU!
SAY *CHEESE*.

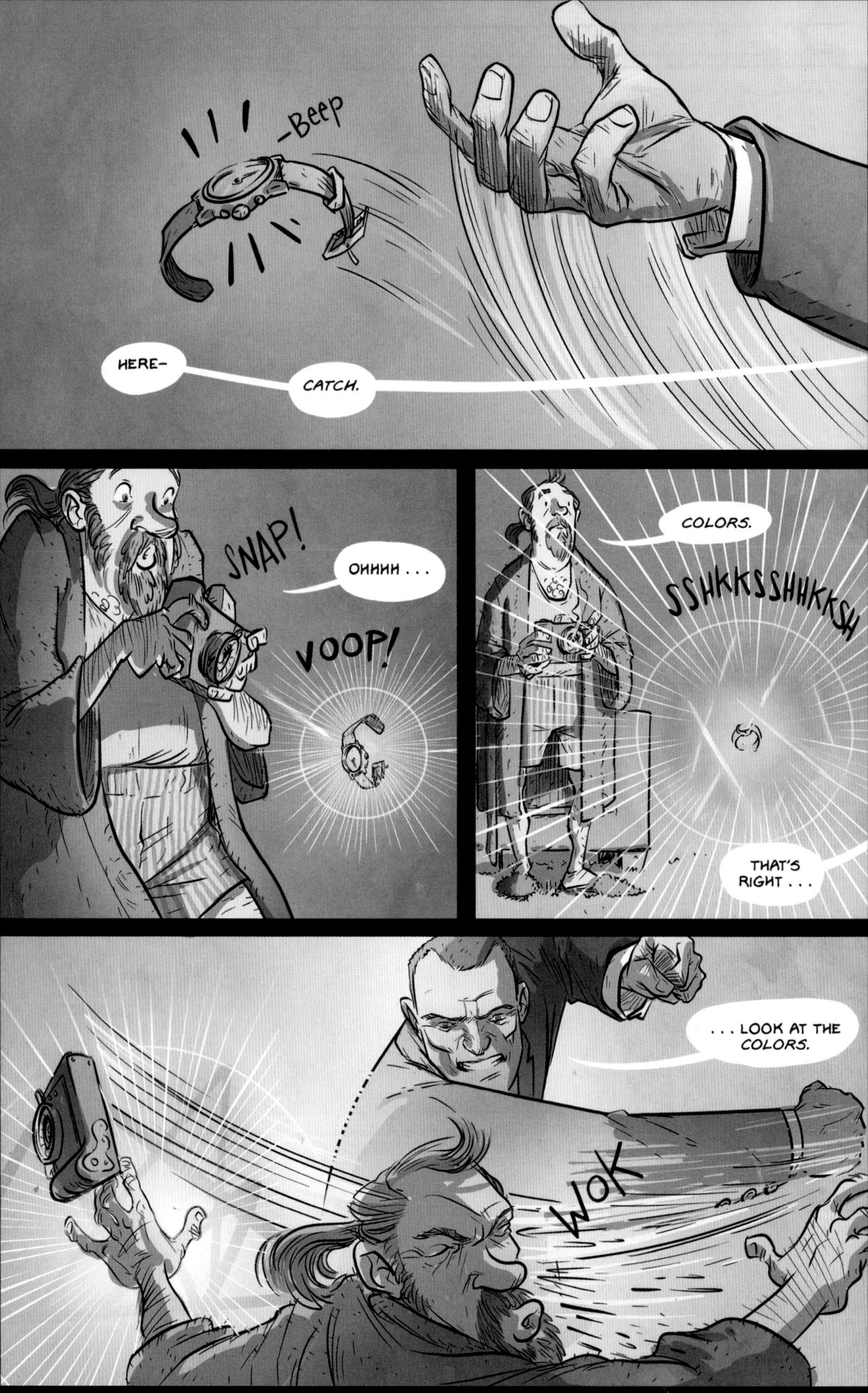
-Beep
HERE-
CATCH.
SNAP!
OHHHH . . .
VOOP!
COLORS.
SSHKKSSHHKKSH
THAT'S RIGHT . . .
. . . LOOK AT THE COLORS.
WOK

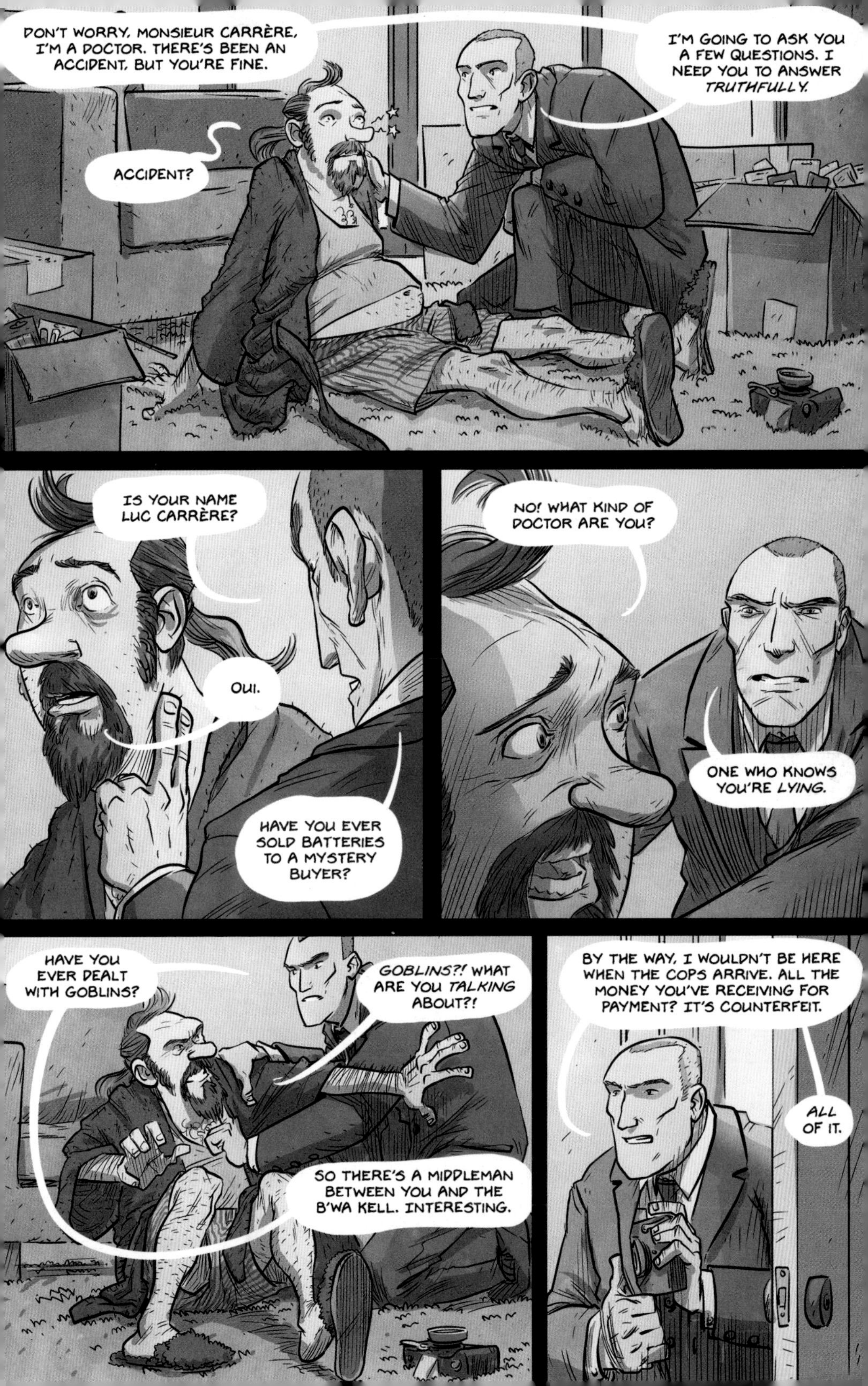
DON'T WORRY, MONSIEUR CARRÈRE, I'M A DOCTOR. THERE'S BEEN AN ACCIDENT, BUT YOU'RE FINE.
I'M GOING TO ASK YOU A FEW QUESTIONS. I NEED YOU TO ANSWER *TRUTHFULLY.*
ACCIDENT?
IS YOUR NAME LUC CARRÈRE?
OUI.
HAVE YOU EVER SOLD BATTERIES TO A MYSTERY BUYER?
NO! WHAT KIND OF DOCTOR ARE YOU?
ONE WHO KNOWS YOU'RE *LYING.*
HAVE YOU EVER DEALT WITH GOBLINS?
GOBLINS?! WHAT ARE YOU *TALKING* ABOUT?!
SO THERE'S A MIDDLEMAN BETWEEN YOU AND THE B'WA KELL. INTERESTING.
BY THE WAY, I WOULDN'T BE HERE WHEN THE COPS ARRIVE. ALL THE MONEY YOU'VE RECEIVING FOR PAYMENT? IT'S COUNTERFEIT.
ALL OF IT.

CHAPTER SEVEN

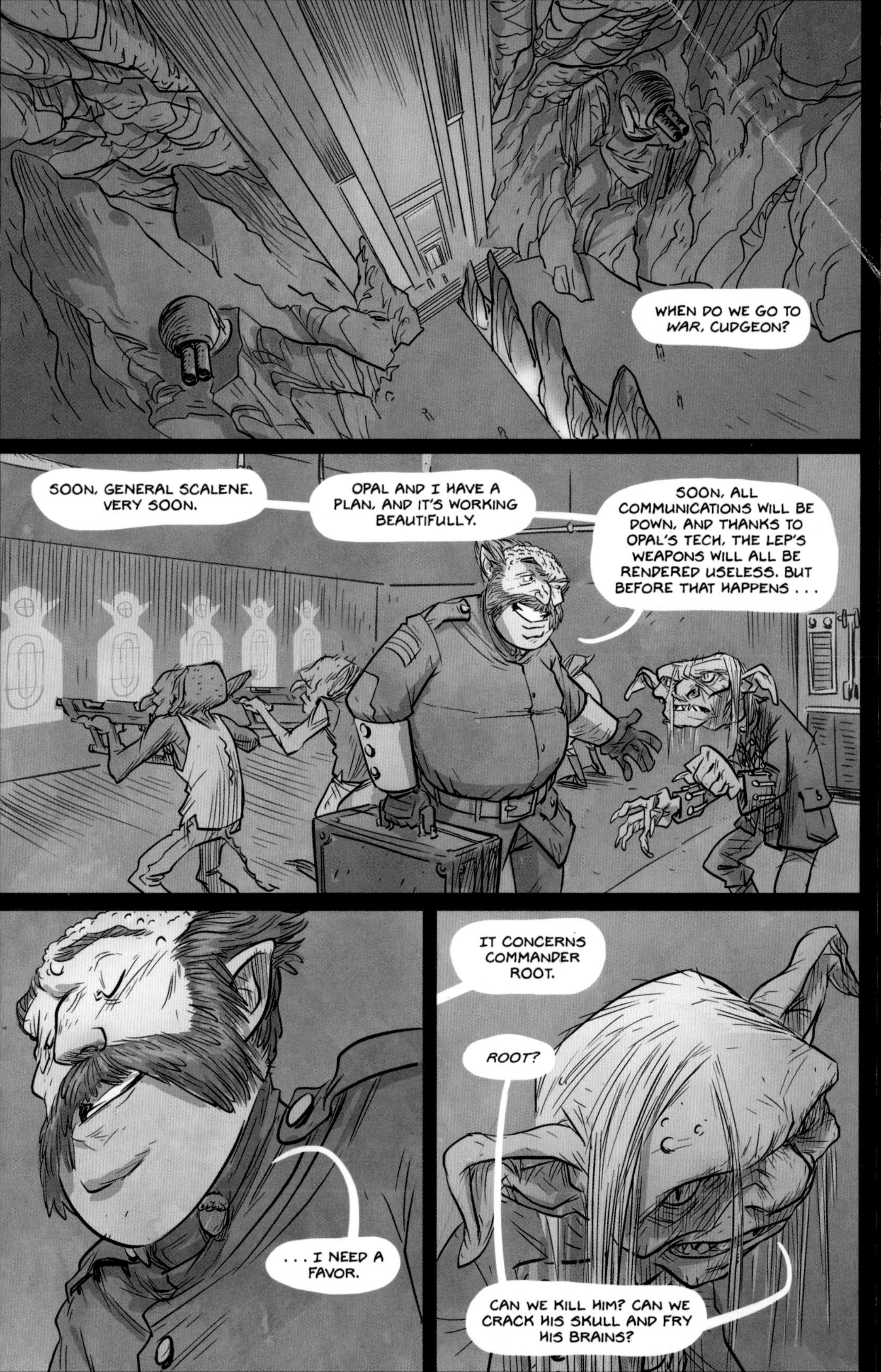
WHEN DO WE GO TO *WAR*, CUDGEON?
SOON, GENERAL SCALENE. VERY SOON.
OPAL AND I HAVE A PLAN, AND IT'S WORKING BEAUTIFULLY.
SOON, ALL COMMUNICATIONS WILL BE DOWN, AND THANKS TO OPAL'S TECH, THE LEP'S WEAPONS WILL ALL BE RENDERED USELESS. BUT BEFORE THAT HAPPENS . . .
. . . I NEED A FAVOR.
IT CONCERNS COMMANDER ROOT.
ROOT?
CAN WE KILL HIM? CAN WE CRACK HIS SKULL AND FRY HIS BRAINS?

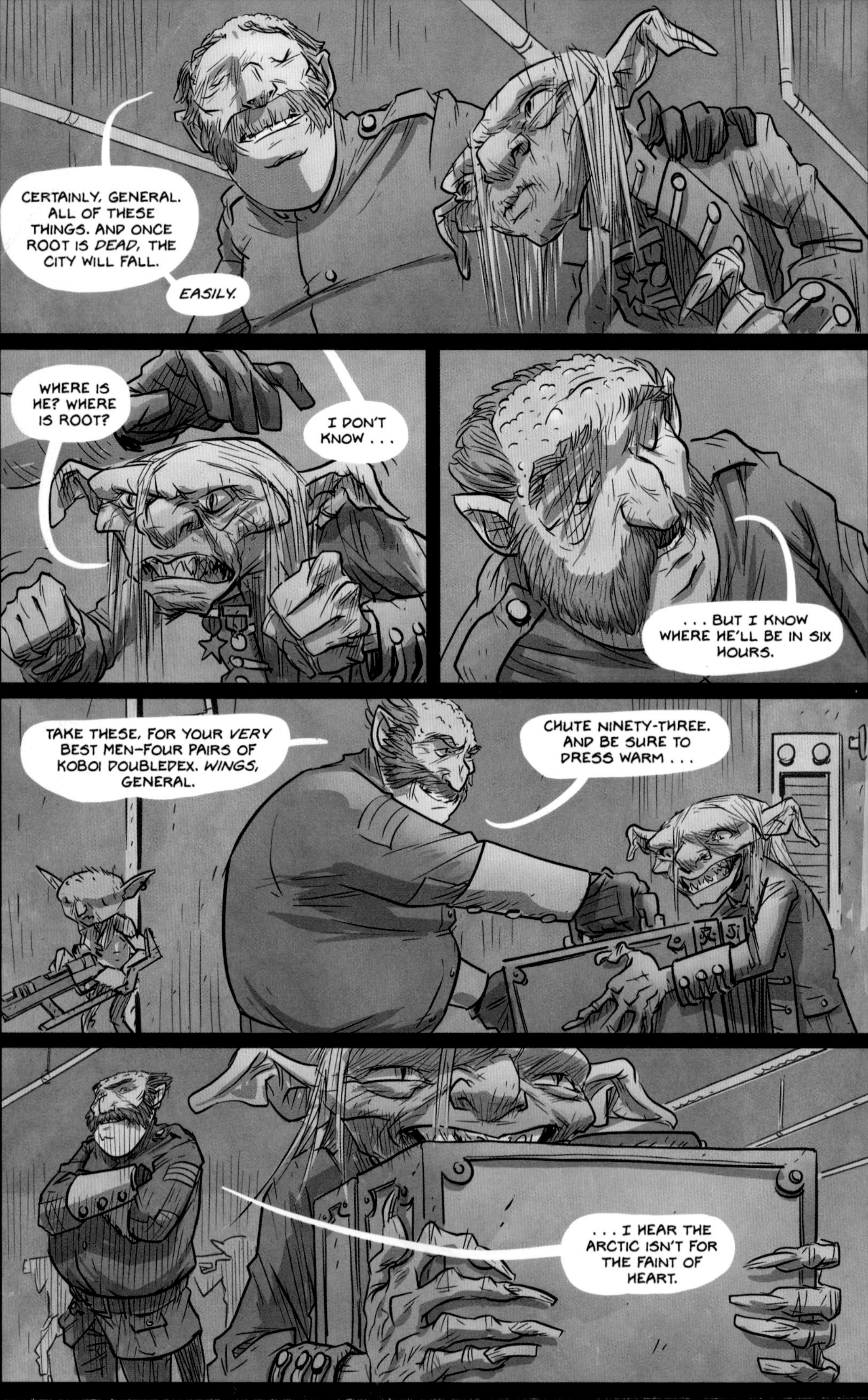
CERTAINLY, GENERAL. ALL OF THESE THINGS. AND ONCE ROOT IS *DEAD*, THE CITY WILL FALL.
EASILY.
WHERE IS HE? WHERE IS ROOT?
I DON'T KNOW . . .
. . . BUT I KNOW WHERE HE'LL BE IN SIX HOURS.
TAKE THESE, FOR YOUR *VERY* BEST MEN—FOUR PAIRS OF KOBOI DOUBLEDEX. *WINGS*, GENERAL.
CHUTE NINETY-THREE. AND BE SURE TO DRESS WARM . . .
. . . I HEAR THE ARCTIC ISN'T FOR THE FAINT OF HEART.

CHAPTER EIGHT

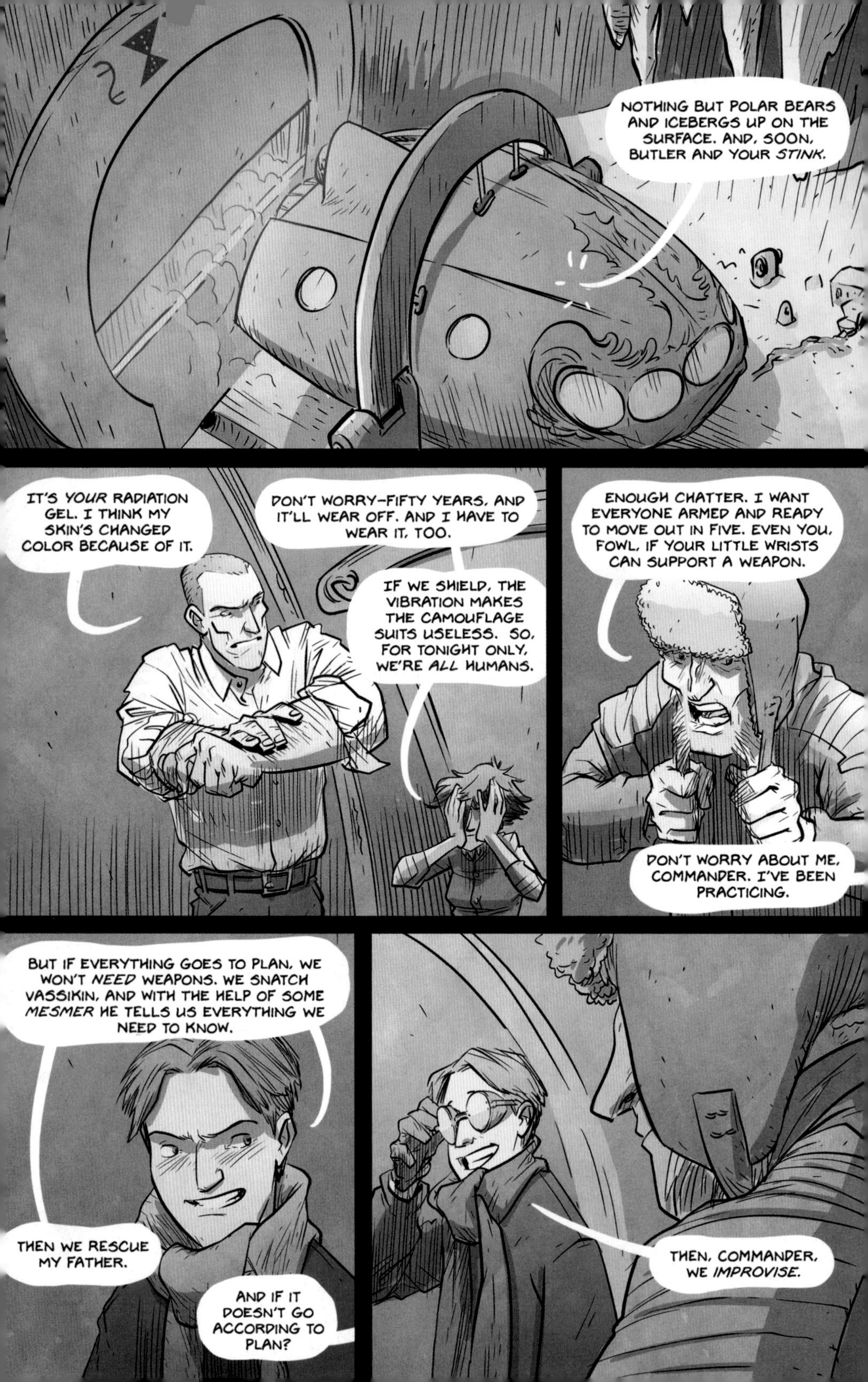
NOTHING BUT POLAR BEARS AND ICEBERGS UP ON THE SURFACE. AND, SOON, BUTLER AND YOUR *STINK*.
IT'S *YOUR* RADIATION GEL. I THINK MY SKIN'S CHANGED COLOR BECAUSE OF IT.
DON'T WORRY—FIFTY YEARS, AND IT'LL WEAR OFF. AND I HAVE TO WEAR IT, TOO.
IF WE SHIELD, THE VIBRATION MAKES THE CAMOUFLAGE SUITS USELESS. SO, FOR TONIGHT ONLY, WE'RE *ALL* HUMANS.
ENOUGH CHATTER. I WANT EVERYONE ARMED AND READY TO MOVE OUT IN FIVE. EVEN YOU, FOWL, IF YOUR LITTLE WRISTS CAN SUPPORT A WEAPON.
DON'T WORRY ABOUT ME, COMMANDER. I'VE BEEN PRACTICING.
BUT IF EVERYTHING GOES TO PLAN, WE WON'T *NEED* WEAPONS. WE SNATCH VASSIKIN, AND WITH THE HELP OF SOME *MESMER* HE TELLS US EVERYTHING WE NEED TO KNOW.
THEN WE RESCUE MY FATHER.
AND IF IT DOESN'T GO ACCORDING TO PLAN?
THEN, COMMANDER, WE *IMPROVISE*.

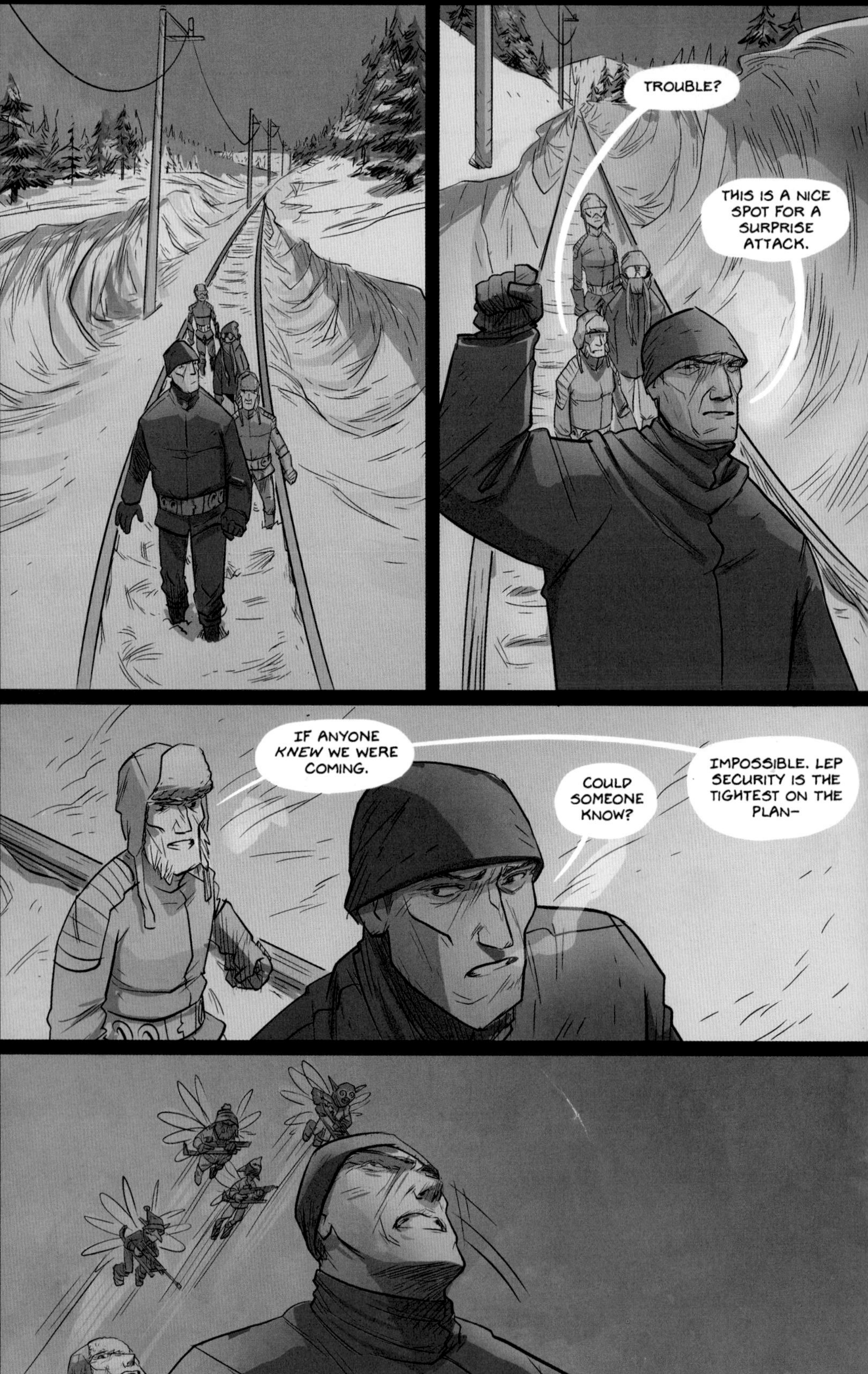
TROUBLE?
THIS IS A NICE SPOT FOR A SURPRISE ATTACK.
IF ANYONE *KNEW* WE WERE COMING.
COULD SOMEONE KNOW?
IMPOSSIBLE. LEP SECURITY IS THE TIGHTEST ON THE PLAN-

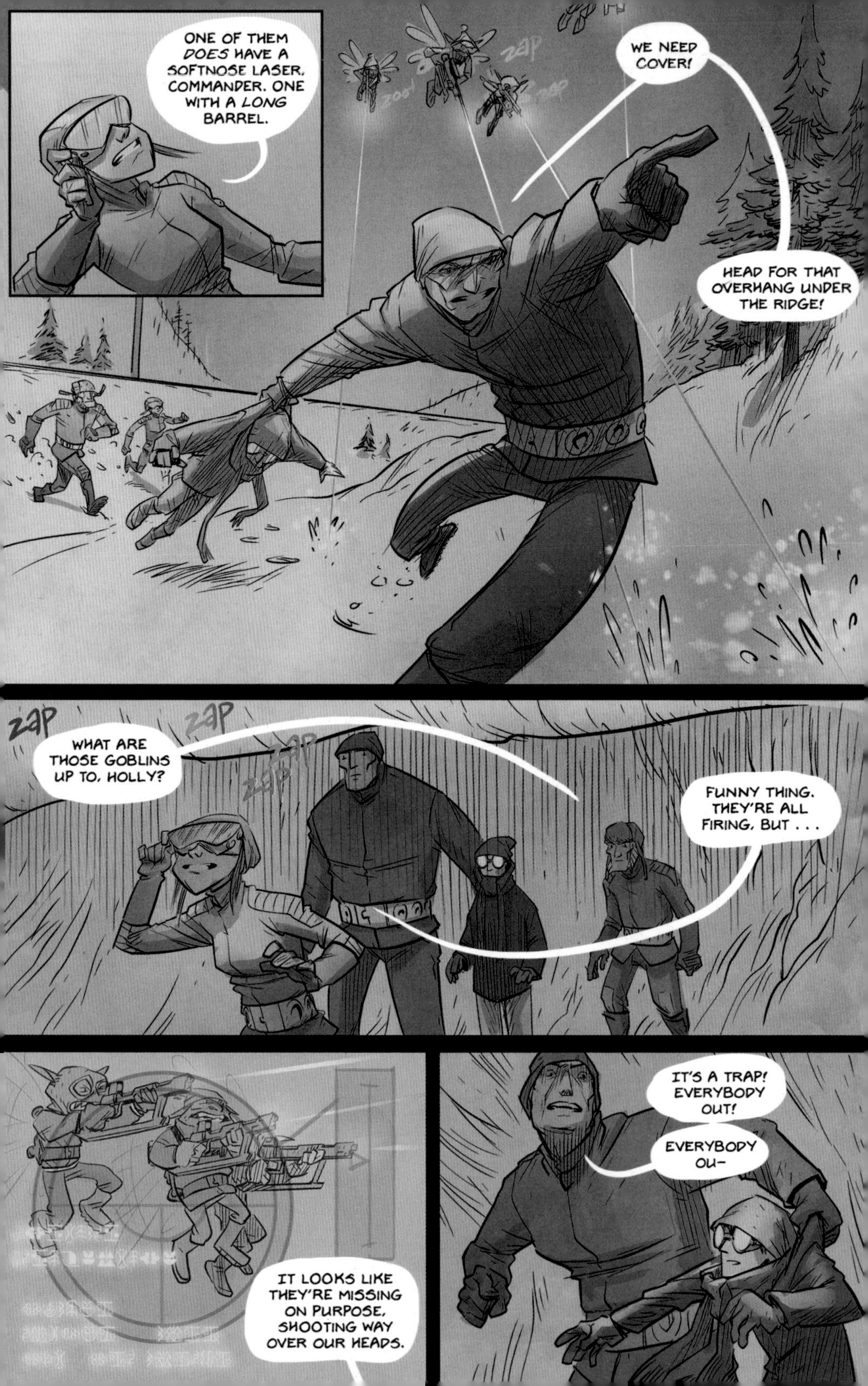
ONE OF THEM DOES HAVE A SOFTNOSE LASER, COMMANDER. ONE WITH A LONG BARREL.
ZAP
WE NEED COVER!
HEAD FOR THAT OVERHANG UNDER THE RIDGE!
ZAP
ZAP
WHAT ARE THOSE GOBLINS UP TO, HOLLY?
ZAP ZAP
FUNNY THING. THEY'RE ALL FIRING, BUT . . .
IT LOOKS LIKE THEY'RE MISSING ON PURPOSE, SHOOTING WAY OVER OUR HEADS.
IT'S A TRAP! EVERYBODY OUT!
EVERYBODY OU-

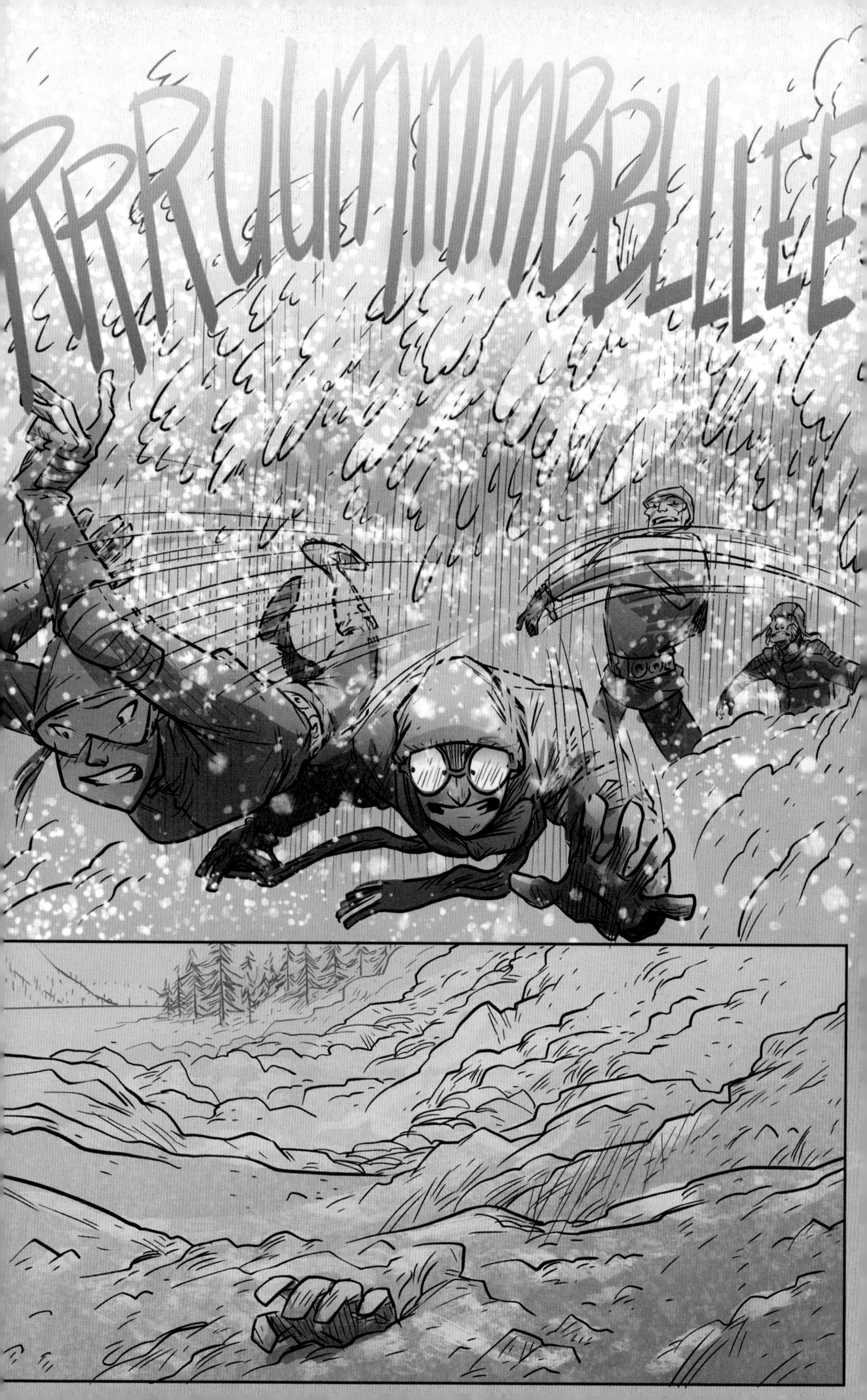
RRRUUMMMBBLLEE

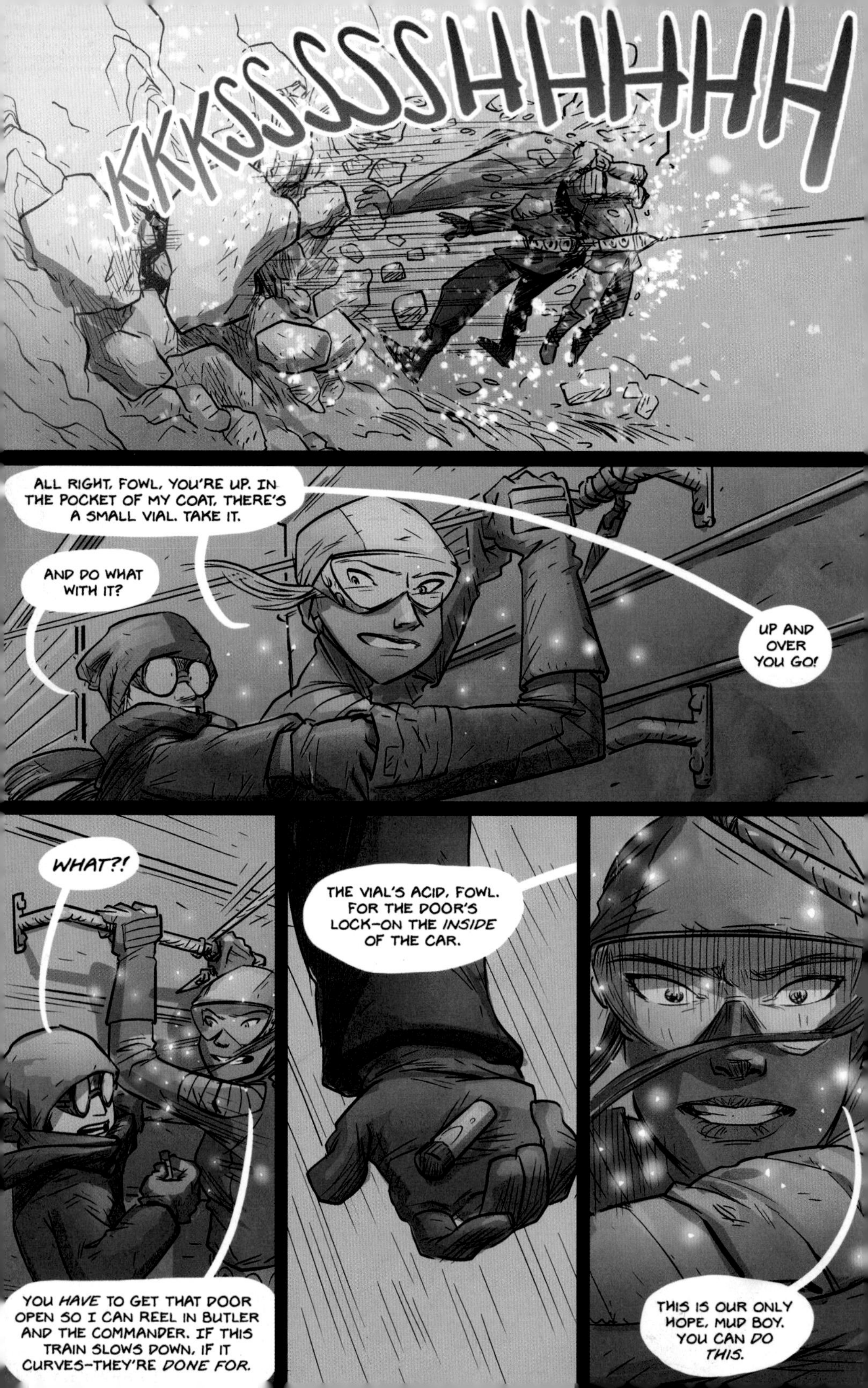
KKKSSSSSHHHHHH
ALL RIGHT, FOWL, YOU'RE UP. IN THE POCKET OF MY COAT, THERE'S A SMALL VIAL. TAKE IT.
AND DO WHAT WITH IT?
UP AND OVER YOU GO!
WHAT?!
YOU *HAVE* TO GET THAT DOOR OPEN SO I CAN REEL IN BUTLER AND THE COMMANDER. IF THIS TRAIN SLOWS DOWN, IF IT CURVES—THEY'RE *DONE FOR.*
THE VIAL'S ACID, FOWL. FOR THE DOOR'S LOCK—ON THE *INSIDE* OF THE CAR.
THIS IS OUR ONLY HOPE, MUD BOY. YOU CAN *DO THIS.*

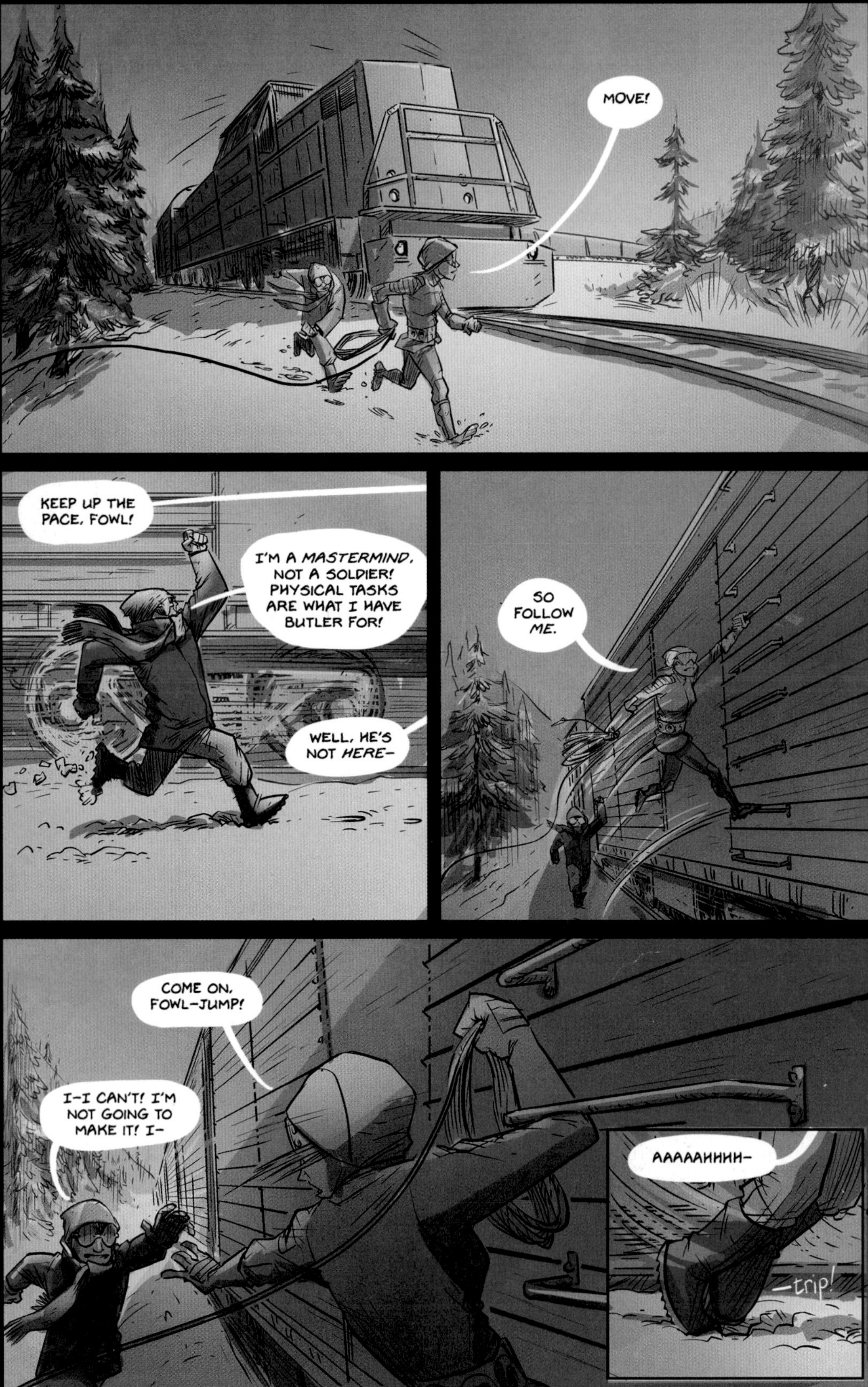
MOVE!
KEEP UP THE PACE, FOWL!
I'M A *MASTERMIND*, NOT A SOLDIER! PHYSICAL TASKS ARE WHAT I HAVE BUTLER FOR!
WELL, HE'S NOT *HERE*–
SO FOLLOW *ME*.
COME ON, FOWL–JUMP!
I–I CAN'T! I'M NOT GOING TO MAKE IT! I–
AAAAAHHH–
–trip!

KKKSSSSSSHHHHH

ALL RIGHT FOWL, YOU'RE UP. IN THE POCKET OF MY COAT, THERE'S A SMALL VIAL. TAKE IT.

AND DO WHAT WITH IT?

UP AND OVER YOU GO!

WHAT?!

YOU *HAVE* TO GET THAT DOOR OPEN SO I CAN REEL IN BUTLER AND THE COMMANDER. IF THIS TRAIN SLOWS DOWN, IF IT CURVES—THEY'RE *DONE* FOR.

THE VIAL'S ACID, FOWL. FOR THE DOOR'S LOCK—ON THE *INSIDE* OF THE CAR.

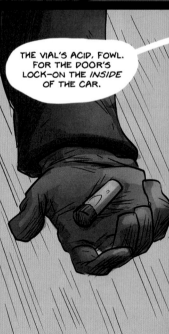

THIS IS OUR ONLY HOPE, MUD BOY. YOU CAN *DO* THIS.

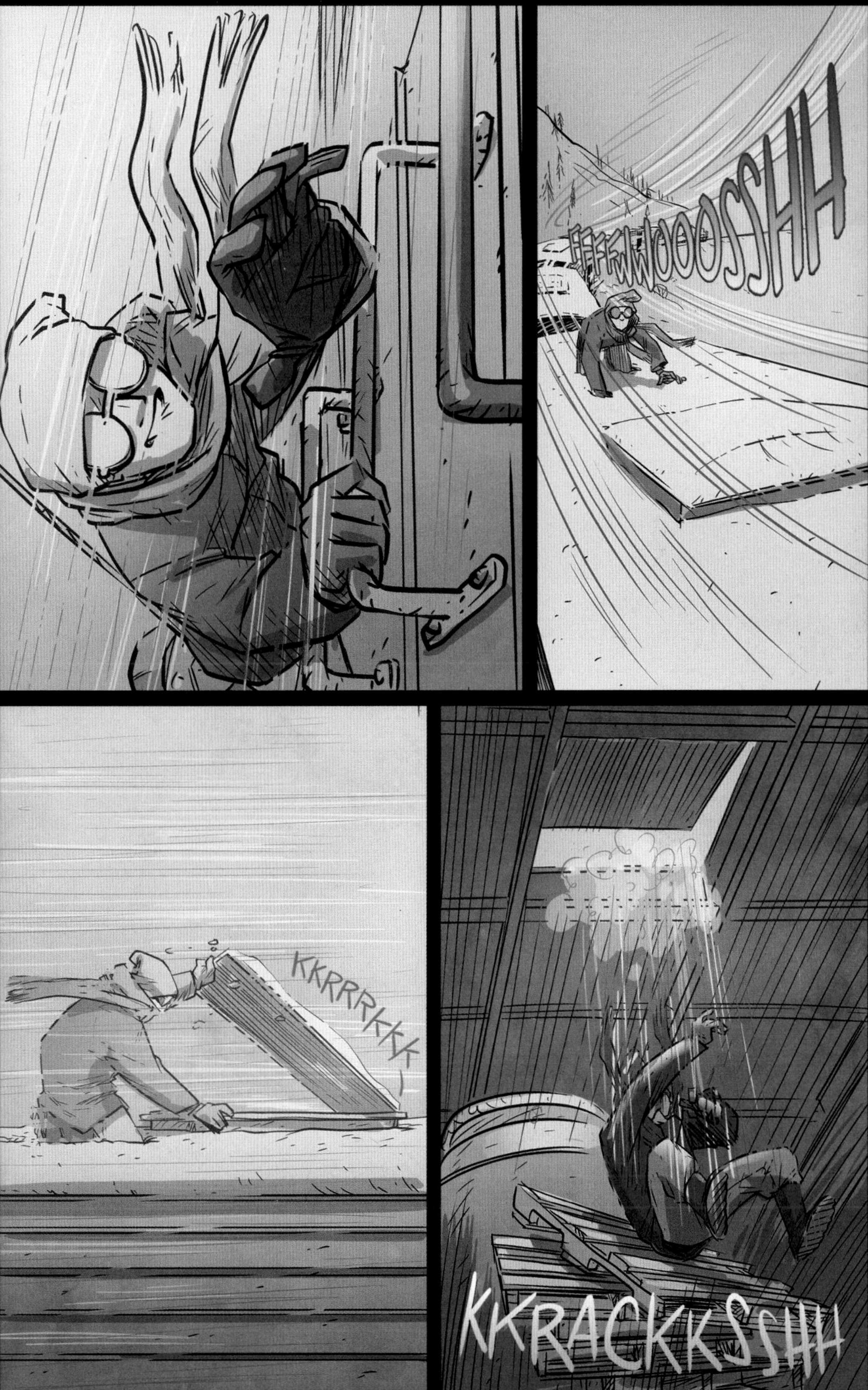
FFFFWWOOOSHH
KKRRRRKKK
KKRACKKSSHH

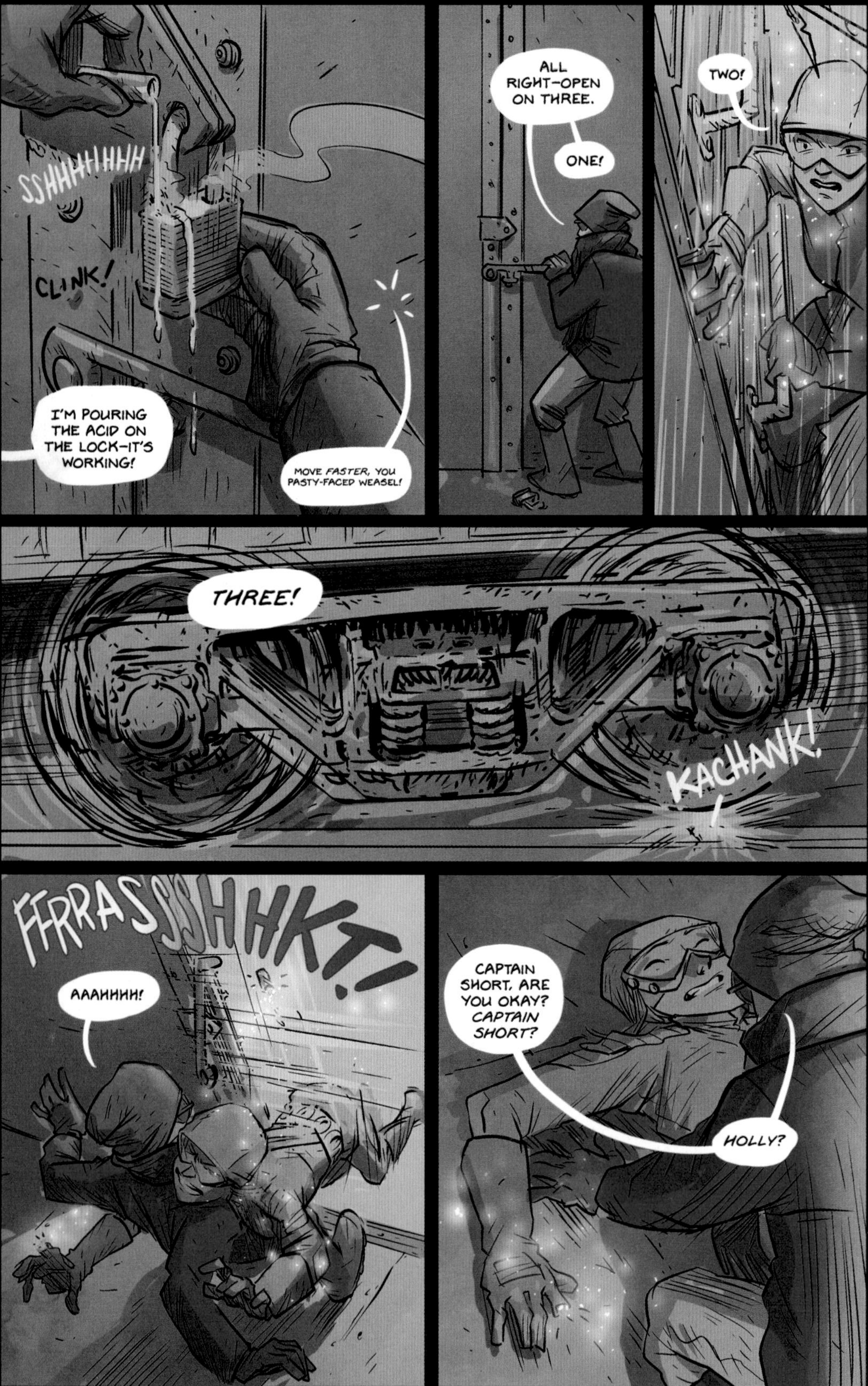
SSHHHHHHH
CLINK!
I'M POURING THE ACID ON THE LOCK—IT'S WORKING!
MOVE FASTER, YOU PASTY-FACED WEASEL!
ALL RIGHT—OPEN ON THREE.
ONE!
TWO!
THREE!
KACHANK!
FFRRASSSHHKT!!
AAAHHHH!
CAPTAIN SHORT, ARE YOU OKAY? CAPTAIN SHORT?
HOLLY?

CHAPTER NINE

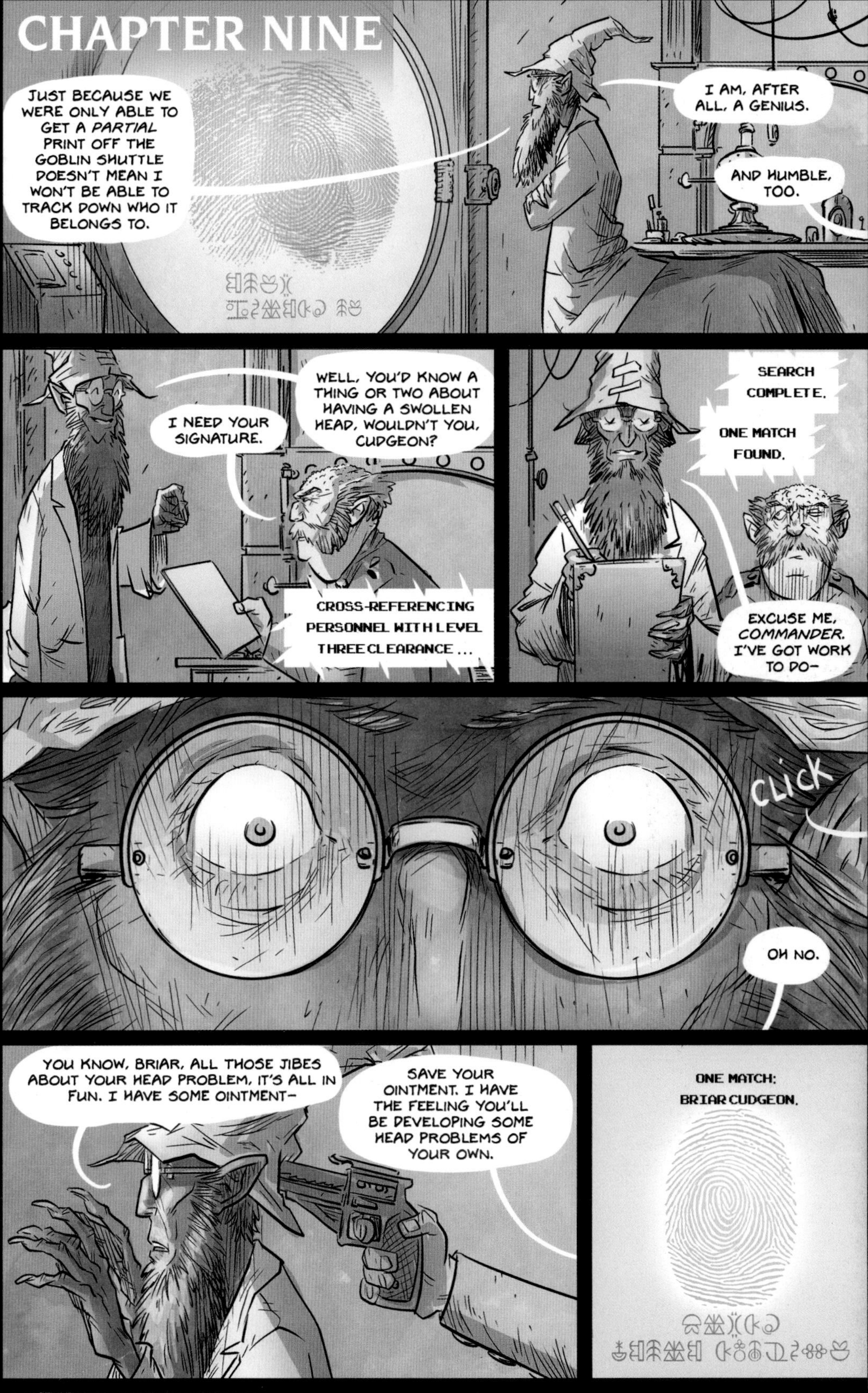
JUST BECAUSE WE WERE ONLY ABLE TO GET A *PARTIAL* PRINT OFF THE GOBLIN SHUTTLE DOESN'T MEAN I WON'T BE ABLE TO TRACK DOWN WHO IT BELONGS TO.
I AM, AFTER ALL, A GENIUS.
AND HUMBLE, TOO.
I NEED YOUR SIGNATURE.
WELL, YOU'D KNOW A THING OR TWO ABOUT HAVING A SWOLLEN HEAD, WOULDN'T YOU, CUDGEON?
CROSS-REFERENCING PERSONNEL WITH LEVEL THREE CLEARANCE . . .
SEARCH COMPLETE.
ONE MATCH FOUND.
EXCUSE ME, *COMMANDER.* I'VE GOT WORK TO DO—
CLICK
OH NO.
YOU KNOW, BRIAR, ALL THOSE JIBES ABOUT YOUR HEAD PROBLEM, IT'S ALL IN FUN. I HAVE SOME OINTMENT—
SAVE YOUR OINTMENT. I HAVE THE FEELING YOU'LL BE DEVELOPING SOME HEAD PROBLEMS OF YOUR OWN.
ONE MATCH:
BRIAR CUDGEON.

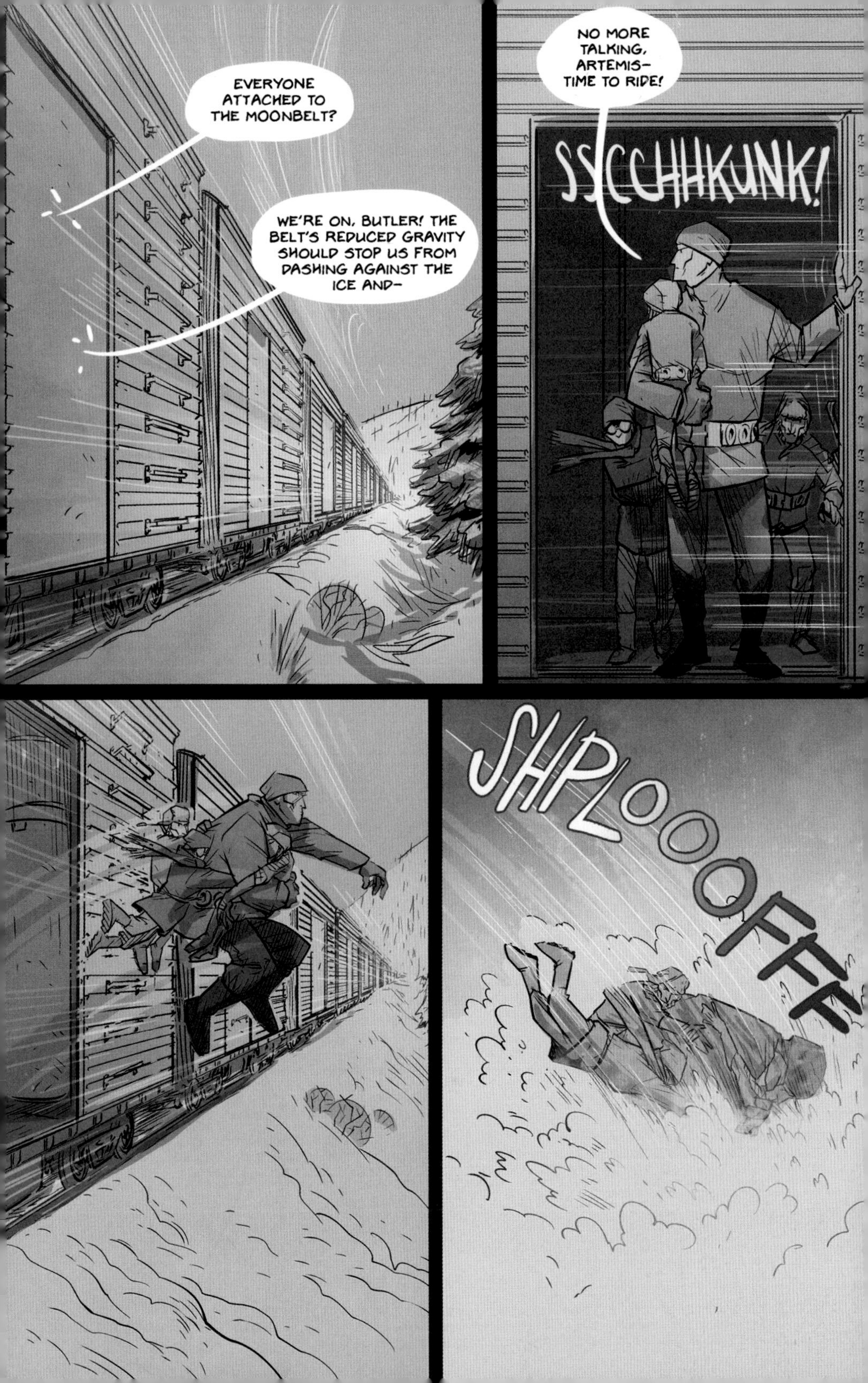
EVERYONE ATTACHED TO THE MOONBELT?
WE'RE ON, BUTLER! THE BELT'S REDUCED GRAVITY SHOULD STOP US FROM DASHING AGAINST THE ICE AND—
NO MORE TALKING, ARTEMIS— TIME TO RIDE!
SSCCHHKUNK!
SHPLOOOFFF

SO WE WERE AMBUSHED BY A B'WA KELL HIT TEAM. WHAT DOES THAT MEAN?

IT MEANS . . .

. . . THAT YOU HAVE A LEAK.

WE KNOW THAT THE GOBLINS HAVE A SOURCE IN THE LEP.

WE KNOW YOUR WEAPONS ARE OUT. AND WE KNOW IF THEY TAKE OUT THE LEP'S HEAD, COMMANDER ROOT, THEY MUST GO AFTER THE BODY AS WELL.

HENCE THE REVOLUTION LIKELY TAKING PLACE IN THE UNDERGROUND.

I SUGGEST WE PROCEED TOWARD MURMANSK AS SOON AS WE GET CLOUD COVER.

BUTLER CAN SEARCH VASSIKIN'S APARTMENT. PERHAPS WE'LL GET LUCKY AND MY FATHER WILL BE THERE.

WE DON'T HAVE WEAPONS, BUT—

ARTEMIS.

WE'RE IN NO *SHAPE* TO GO AGAINST THE MAFIYA.

IF WE GO IN THERE *NOW*, NONE OF US ARE MAKING IT BACK OUT.

BUT MY FATHER IS SO *CLOSE*. I CAN'T GIVE UP NOW.

NO ONE IS GIVING UP. WE'RE REGROUPING.

REMEMBER—IT'S ALWAYS DARKEST BEFORE THE DAWN.

WHAT DAWN?

WE'RE IN THE ARCTIC, REMEMBER?

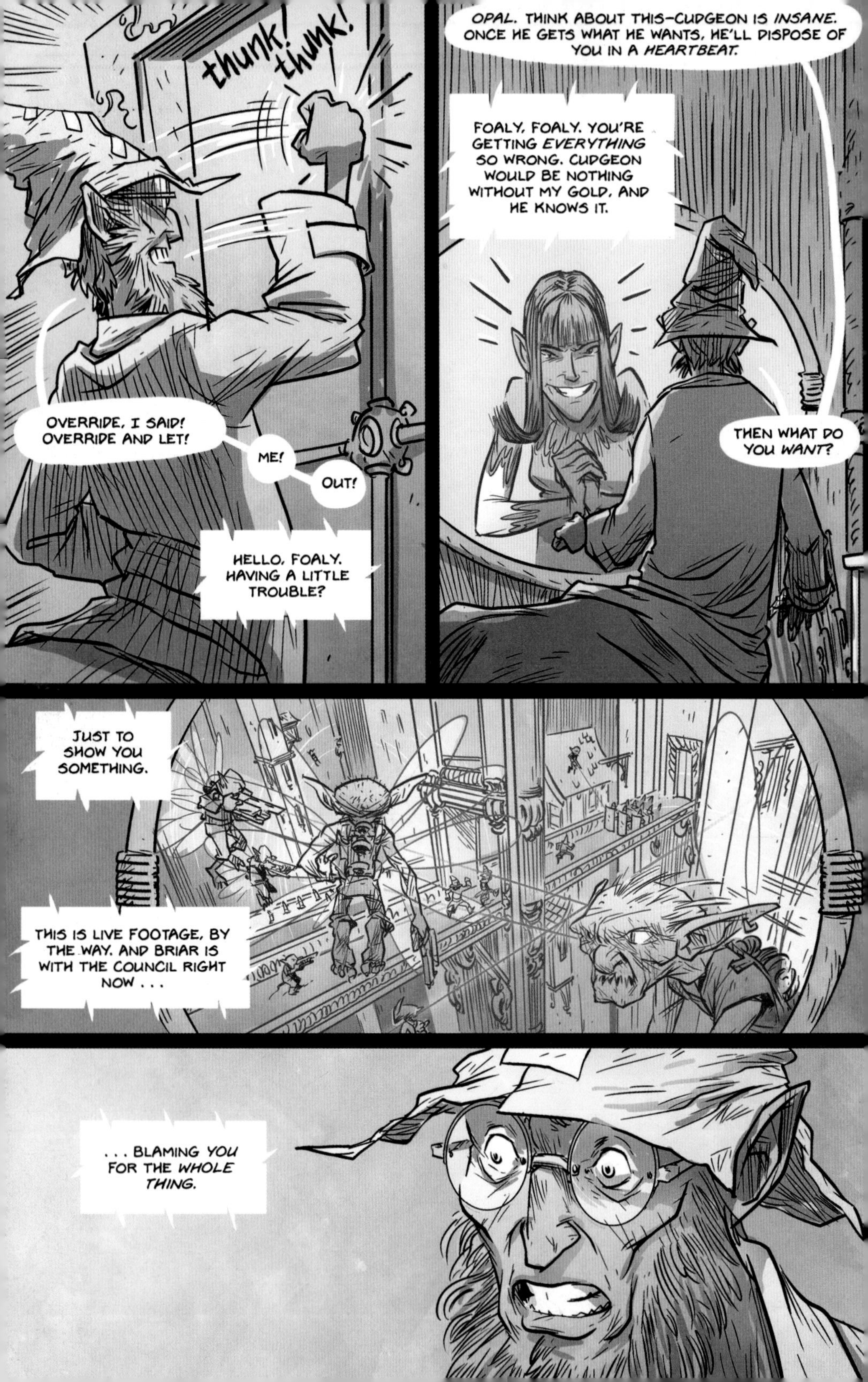
thunk! thunk!
OVERRIDE, I SAID! OVERRIDE AND LET!
ME!
OUT!
HELLO, FOALY. HAVING A LITTLE TROUBLE?
OPAL. THINK ABOUT THIS—CUDGEON IS *INSANE*. ONCE HE GETS WHAT HE WANTS, HE'LL DISPOSE OF YOU IN A *HEARTBEAT*.
FOALY, FOALY. YOU'RE GETTING *EVERYTHING* SO WRONG. CUDGEON WOULD BE NOTHING WITHOUT MY GOLD, AND HE KNOWS IT.
THEN WHAT DO YOU *WANT*?
JUST TO SHOW YOU SOMETHING.
THIS IS LIVE FOOTAGE, BY THE WAY. AND BRIAR IS WITH THE COUNCIL RIGHT NOW . . .
. . . BLAMING *YOU* FOR THE *WHOLE* THING.

CHAPTER TEN

CHAPTER ELEVEN

CHAPTER TWELVE

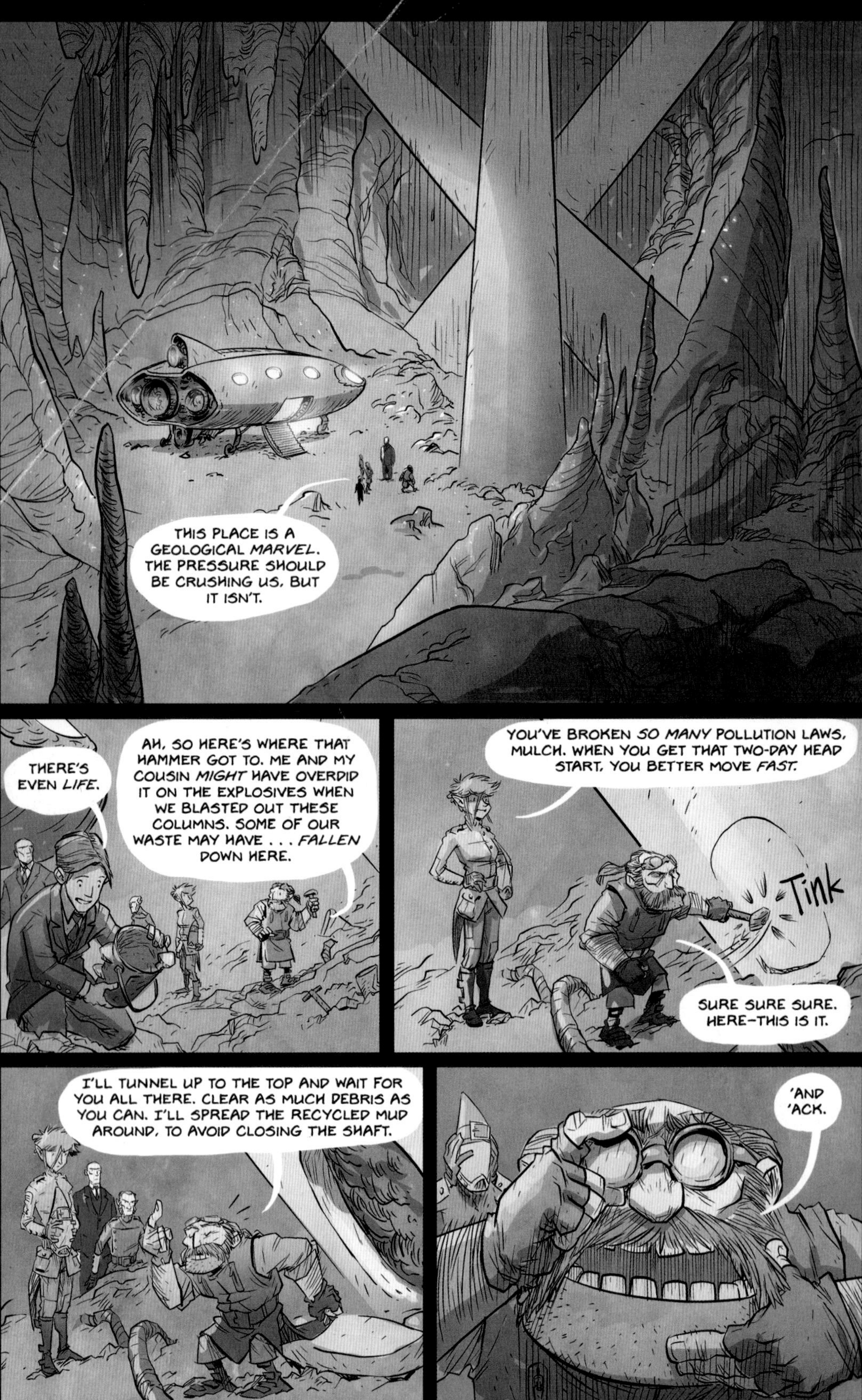
THIS PLACE IS A GEOLOGICAL *MARVEL*. THE PRESSURE SHOULD BE CRUSHING US, BUT IT ISN'T.
THERE'S EVEN *LIFE*.
AH, SO HERE'S WHERE THAT HAMMER GOT TO. ME AND MY COUSIN *MIGHT* HAVE OVERDID IT ON THE EXPLOSIVES WHEN WE BLASTED OUT THESE COLUMNS. SOME OF OUR WASTE MAY HAVE . . . *FALLEN* DOWN HERE.
YOU'VE BROKEN *SO MANY* POLLUTION LAWS, MULCH. WHEN YOU GET THAT TWO-DAY HEAD START, YOU BETTER MOVE *FAST*.
TINK
SURE SURE SURE. HERE—THIS IS IT.
I'LL TUNNEL UP TO THE TOP AND WAIT FOR YOU ALL THERE. CLEAR AS MUCH DEBRIS AS YOU CAN. I'LL SPREAD THE RECYCLED MUD AROUND, TO AVOID CLOSING THE SHAFT.
'AND 'ACK.

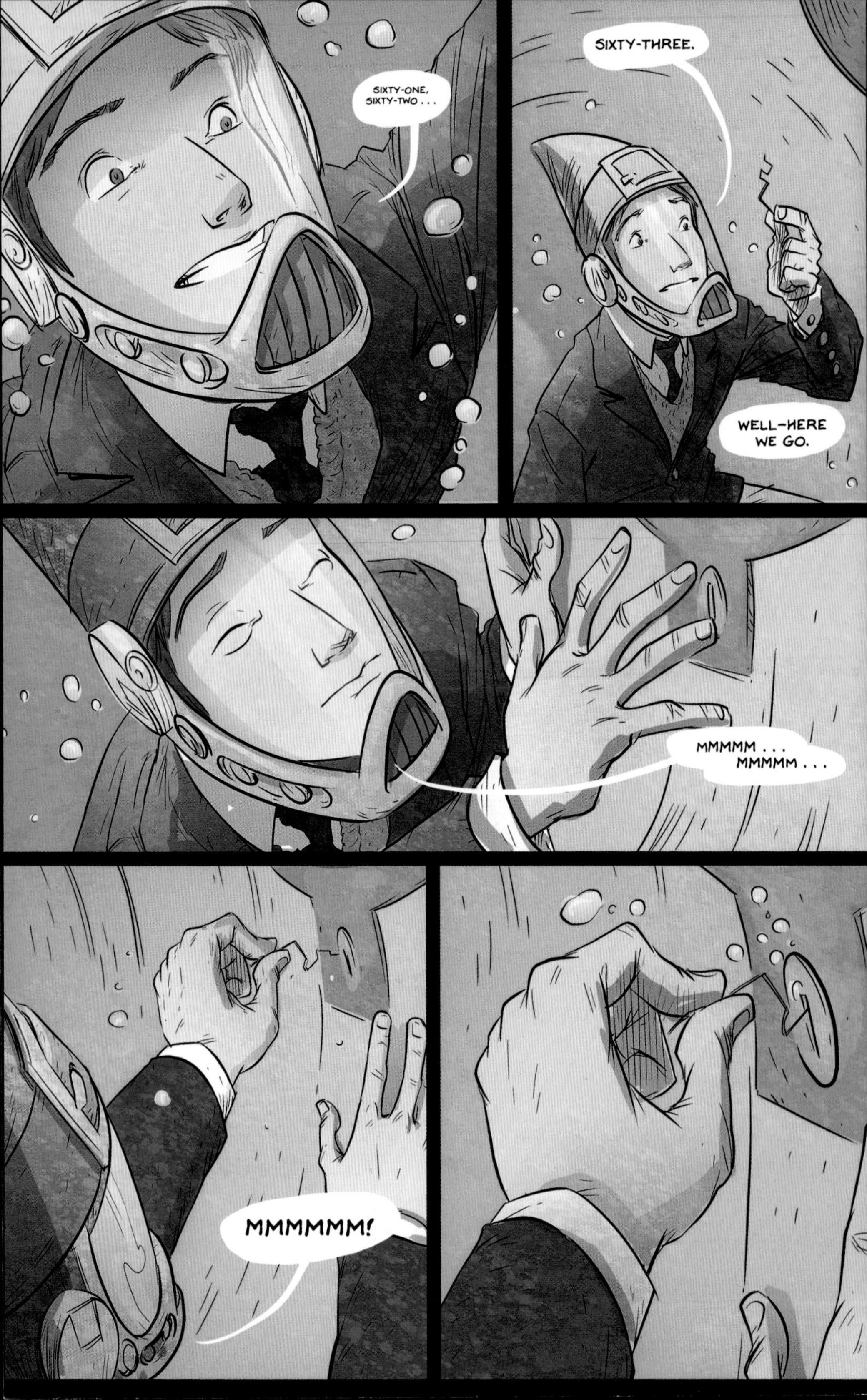
SIXTY-ONE, SIXTY-TWO . . .
SIXTY-THREE.
WELL—HERE WE GO.
MMMMM . . . MMMMM . . .
MMMMMM!

HE SHOT HIM!

THAT DEVIL SHOT HIS OWN FATHER!

SPLish!

IDIOT! NOW OUR HOSTAGE IS OVERBOARD!

DO YOU THINK HE'S DEAD?

HE WAS BLEEDING BADLY. IF THE BULLET DOESN'T FINISH HIM, THE WATER WILL. ANYWAY, IT'S NOT OUR FAULT.

I DON'T THINK BRITVA WILL SEE IT THAT WAY.

YOU CRAZY DEVIL, FOWL! YOUR FATHER IS AS GOOD AS DEAD—I THOUGHT WE HAD A DEAL!

WE STILL DO. A NEW ONE. SEE, THE LAST THING I NEED IS FOR MY FATHER TO RETURN AND DESTROY WHAT I'VE BUILT WHILE HE WAS GONE.

HE HAD TO DIE.

YOU CAN HAVE THE RANSOM MONEY. IN EXCHANGE, I GET SAFE PASSAGE HOME. FAIR ENOUGH?

SEEMS FAIR TO ME.

LOOK ACROSS THE BAY, ABOVE THE FJORD. YOU'LL SEE A FLARE. IT GOES OUT IN TEN MINUTES.

I'D GET THERE BEFORE THE FIRE DIES.

WELL?

THE MONEY. UP THERE, BY THE FLARE. WE'RE RICH.

EPILOGUE